THE BOY BIGGLES

THE BOY BIGGLES

by
CAPT. W. E. JOHNS

PRINTED IN GREAT BRITAIN
DEAN & SON Ltd
41/43 Ludgate Hill   LONDON EC4

MADE AND PRINTED IN GREAT BRITAIN BY PURNELL AND SONS LTD
PAULTON (SOMERSET) AND LONDON

603 03401 2

CONTENTS

A WORD IN ADVANCE

Most healthy boys have an inborn appetite for adventure. If it does not come to them they will go out to look for it. It is the urge which from the beginning of history has sent men out to explore the unknown, to climb hostile mountains, to sail dangerous seas, in fact to do anything that involves a risk to life. Why do they do it? Is it prompted by curiosity? The hope of a thrill? A test of nerve, to prove something? If this impulsion is not satisfied it may stay with a man all his life. If all else fails he may find consolation from reading about the adventures of others.

Had it not been for this impulse much of the world would still remain unexplored. Men have accepted the challenge of the seemingly impossible apparently for no other reason than to prove something could be done. It took them to the Poles although there was nothing there—not even a pole!

The sort of adventure the average boy hopes to find must of course depend on where he lives. If there are rocks he will scale them. If there are caves he is likely to go pot-holing. If there are trees he will climb them. If there is a dangerous river near at hand it is there he will be found. There is seldom any practical purpose in doing any of these things.

Danger is the magnet. If there is no danger there is no adventure. The greater the danger the greater the satisfaction of success.

In so-called civilized countries a boy may have to go out of his way to find an exercise to challenge his nerves. He may walk on an icebound pond merely to see if it will carry his weight. He will climb a cliff for no better reason than to look for a bird's nest or swim in a river said to have dangerous currents to see if it is true. Why he should so risk losing his life we don't know. It is unlikely that he himself knows. But the fact remains, he does; he always has, and presumably always will. It is part of the human make-up.

If a boy happens to live in a tropical climate with virgin forest or jungle around him he need seldom go far to find excitement. It is more likely to come to him, and that can happen anywhere, at any moment. In most of the remaining forests of Europe a boy may walk carefree in the assurance that he will emerge alive. Not so in the great jungle area where Biggles was born. There, death could lurk at any corner, pounce from behind the next bush, or, in the case of a poisonous snake, lie like a dead stick across the path for the unwary to step on.

In India thousands of people die every year from accidental encounters with wild creatures, and that does not include snake-bite, which accounts for the highest number of fatalities. A single man-eating tiger has been known to kill two hundred people in one village. A deadly little snake called the *krait* is even found in urban districts. Wherefore it becomes instinctive for a boy to look where he is going and where he is putting his feet. He also learns to look up, for a thirty-foot python can drop from a tree on an unsuspecting prey. If he is wise he will have a good hard look at a stream, before he steps into it, for the protruding eyes of a lurking crocodile seeking its next meal.

In short, the hazards to life from traffic in a city are in the wild replaced by dangers from nature in the raw. In either case, if a boy wishes to go on living he must walk carefully. The risks are unavoidable, so must be accepted. In India young James Bigglesworth learned to live with those which he knew were there.

But during the British occupation of India it was an unseen menace which took the greatest toll of human life. Disease. It was fever that filled the churchyards with the white population, particularly the young. It nearly killed Biggles, and probably would have done had he not been sent to the cooler climate of England to give his blood a chance to thicken.

It might be going too far to say that his successful career as a combat pilot was the result of his boy-hood adventures; but that the life he led, with danger never far away, contributed, is not to be doubted. In order to survive he had to learn to use his head, think and act swiftly in a situation where a mistake, or a moment of carelessness, could prove fatal.

He had certain advantages. In the first place he had expert tuition, sometimes being allowed to go out with an experienced *shikari*—that is, hunter—brown or white. While still a small boy, for his own safety he was taught, under strict discipline, the use and care of firearms. At the age of seven he could shoot fast and straight. He had his own light rifle and a sixteen-bore shotgun. It should be said he never went hunting for sport, or for the "pot". The idea of killing something simply to put its stuffed body in a glass case made no appeal to him. He realized that everything had the right to live.

On the occasions when he went out with his rifle it was strictly business. If the depredations of a savage marauder demanded its extermination for the good of the community he was prepared to do it, and without shedding "crocodile" tears over it, either. Later, when he found himself at war it was perhaps natural he should adhere to that policy.

The regular readers of the Biggles books may sometimes have wondered what Biggles was like when he was a boy in India, before he ever saw England. The following pages may provide the answer, or at least help the reader to form an opinion.

A TEST OF NERVE

THE year was 1912. The bungalow of the Assistant Commissioner of the United Provinces of India sweltered under the sultry heat of the approaching monsoon. Vegetation wilted. The fronds of the palms, like the flag on the pole, hung limp and lifeless.

In a room furnished as an office, under the monotonous swinging of a *punkah* that kept the stagnant air moving, two men were talking. One, a tired-looking man of late middle age, immaculate in white, was the Assistant Commissioner himself: Bigglesworth *sahib* of the Indian Civil Service. The other was perhaps a little younger, carelessly dressed in jungle shirt, jodhpurs and high mosquito boots. Present also was a boy with serious, thoughtful eyes. He listened attentively but took no part in the conversation. The senior of the two men was his father; the other, Captain John Lovell of the Indian Army, a celebrated *shikari*, known throughout the Provinces as a destroyer of man-eating tigers and leopards.

To the boy, James Bigglesworth, who until now knew him only by reputation, this mighty hunter was a hero to worship. It was to see him in person that he had asked permission to be present. This had been granted with the usual admonition that he refrained from asking questions. Hence his silence.

His father was talking. "How are you feeling now, Jack? I hear you've been pretty poorly."

The soldier brushed off the question with a smile. "Me? I'm as right as rain—well, that is, almost. I'm as fit as a fiddle at the moment, anyway."

"What was the trouble? The usual fever?"

"I'm afraid it was rather more than that. I'd had several nasty bouts and neglected to do anything about it. You know how it is. The result was a spot of heart trouble. Damned painful, but nothing that can't be put right. The doctor has given me some pills. I have to carry them with me—confounded nuisance. If I feel another attack coming on all I have to do is slip one in my mouth. But you asked me to look in. Any particular reason?"

"Well, I had; but it can wait till you're really on your feet."

"Don't worry about me. I'm all right. What was the trouble?"

"Tiger."

"Where?"

"Cungit village. About five miles in the hills."

"I know it. How long has this been going on?"

"Six weeks. Up to date the villain has taken seven women and two children. He's got bold enough to snatch people from their houses. The village is in a panic. Real reign of terror. No one dare go out. Animals inside with their owners. They're starving for want of fodder. Every door bolted and barricaded."

"Who's the headman? Can't he do something about it?"

"Apparently he's lost his nerve with the rest although in the ordinary way he doesn't lack courage. Nice old boy named Hamid Lal. The usual story has got around that this is no normal man-eater but one that carries an evil demon on its back to warn it of danger. So it's no use trying to kill it. Once this superstitious nonsense starts it becomes a disease that can't be cured. Already they say that for size and ferocity there has never been anything like this brute. It's said to be as big as a buffalo."

"Hamid Lal? Wasn't he the man who recently got a medal for something?" queried Captain Lovell.

"That's right. He was walking down a jungle path with Barnes of the Forestry Service when a tiger sprang out, got Barnes by the shoulder and dragged him down. The rifle was knocked out of his hands. Hamid Lal ran in and picked it up. Naturally, the safety catch was on. He didn't know how to work it, whereupon he used the rifle as a club and beat the tiger across the skull with such good effect that it dropped Barnes and made off."

"Great show. So the government gave him a medal."

"And a pension for life."

The boy spoke. "Bravo. But if he wasn't afraid of a tiger then why should he be so scared of this one?"

"This is a different matter altogether," answered his father. "This scourge is no ordinary tiger. A demon on its back makes it invulnerable—so they believe. You'll learn that once these people get the idea that a beast is possessed with supernatural powers, in this case the spirit of a dead murderer, their nerve melts like ice in the sun. That's what centuries of superstition have done to them. This fear is infectious, and I'm afraid Hamid Lal, brave man though he is, has succumbed with the rest."

"Have you done anything about it?" inquired Lovell.

"I sent word to Hamid Lal to build a *machan* near the village thinking you might like to sit up over a bait and catch this pest when he makes another raid; but since you're on the sick list I wouldn't——"

"Forget it," broke in the soldier. "I'm not so sick that I can't handle this. Leave it to me. I'll go right along and get everything ready for to-night."

The boy spoke again, looking startled by his temerity. "May I come with you, sir?"

His father answered, curtly. "Certainly not. You're too young for this sort of thing. Besides, you'd be in the way."

Captain Lovell smiled. "How old are you, James?"

"Twelve, sir."

"That's all right," the Captain told the older man. "If he's ever going to be a *shikari* the sooner he picks up a few tips the better. He'll be all right with me. There's nothing dangerous in sitting up in a *machan*." (A platform built in a tree.)

The Commissioner looked doubtful.

"Please let me go, father," urged the boy. "I promise to do everything I'm told."

"I'll see he comes to no harm," Captain Lovell said confidently.

"Very well," agreed the older man, reluctantly. "Keep well wrapped up or we shall have you down again with another dose of fever." Turning to the hunter he explained: "He can't stay in this climate much longer. I'm arranging for him to go to school in England."

"All the more reason why he should see how we deal with wicked tigers before he goes," declared Captain Lovell.

"Shall I bring my rifle?" asked James eagerly.

"No. You won't need it. Mine will be enough."

"As you wish, sir."

"All right. If that's settled we'd better get started to reach the village before dark. It's a fair way. Sure you'll be able to manage it?"

"Easily. No trouble about that, sir."

"Good. Then let's be on our way."

Once out of the township and the cultivated area around it the track to the stricken village wound up steadily rising ground through jungle and forest. To walk through such country was no new experience for James. He loved the untamed wilds, and from frequent hikes with a retired Gond *shikari* on the household staff he knew a good deal about it and was able to identify most things by their native names. There was no danger, of course, ruling out anything as unusual as an unprovoked attack by a large animal or venomous snake. Captain Lovell walked in front, rifle under arm and haversack and water-bottle slung over his shoulders. There was little talking.

Bathed in perspiration, for the atmosphere under the trees was hot and humid, they reached their destination about four o'clock without seeing a soul. The village, a single street of one- or two-roomed clay and wattled huts, lay silent and apparently deserted; every door and window shut.

"They might have come out to meet us, sir," James said.

"Not with a man-eater on the prowl and no better weapon than an ancient *bundook* and perhaps a couple of cartridges. In the ordinary way these people don't lack for courage, but not when a beast has a devil on its back to protect it. As your father said, superstitions about tigers are born in them. And you needn't keep saying sir. Just call me Skipper." Captain Lovell shouted for the headman.

A door opened and after an apprehensive look around an old man came out. His name, he said, was Hamid Lal.

"When did you last see the tiger?" asked Captain Lovell.

The man said it had seized a woman the previous evening. Her goat had got out. She had gone after it. The goat had returned; but not the woman. They had heard her screams.

"Did you build the *machan*?"

Yes. All the men making a great noise had done it that morning. He would show them. Hamid Lal took them along a path perhaps a hundred yards to a clearing in the jungle. In it stood a single tree. In its branches about twelve feet up had been built a simple platform. To reach this some sticks had been lashed at right angles to the trunk to form a ladder. A little to one side of the tree a stake had been driven into the ground as a tethering post. On the fringe of the jungle a nasty mess of blood and rags showed where the tiger's last victim had been killed and devoured.

"Good," said Captain Lovell. "We shall need a goat."

Hamid Lal said they could have the one that had been the cause of the wretched woman's death.

They returned to the village, and as it was rather early to start operations they stayed with the head-man in his house, drinking tea, until the short twilight was beginning to dim the scene outside. Hamid Lal talked in whispers about the dreaded beast, but all they learned from him was that there was nothing regular about its habits. Sometimes it came early, sometimes late. It was bold enough to come into the village, smelling and scratching on the doors. It knew nothing could harm it.

"We'll see about that," Captain Lovell said grimly. "Come on, James, it's time we were getting into position." He picked up the rifle and the water-bottle. "We shan't need the haversack; it can remain here."

Hamid Lal fetched the goat, held by a length of grass rope round its neck, and they set off for the *machan*. There was not a villager in sight. Every door was shut. The headman excused himself from going with them. They heard his door slam and the big wooden bolt thrust home; and James realized what it meant for a village to be under the spell of a striped monster which the people believed nothing could destroy.

With the goat tethered to the post they climbed up on to the *machan* and made themselves as comfortable as the limited space would allow. Captain Lovell sat cross-legged with the rifle on his knees. He took a small electric torch from his pocket and put it handy. "No more talking," he said. "If the old devil hears voices he may suspect a trap. They get crafty when they take to murder."

The darkness closed in. The moon, a misty halo, appeared above the treetops. The edge of a black cloud crept towards it.

"If that confounded cloud starts to spill some rain it'll spoil us," muttered Captain Lovell. "We shan't be able to see or hear a thing. On a still night one can hear a tiger coming as his tail drags through dead leaves."

Nothing more was said. The hush of night settled over the forest. Slowly the cloud crawled across the face of the moon and utter darkness fell

from the sky like a blanket. James stared down into
the black vault below straining his eyes to pick out
a definite object. He could just make out the vague
outline of the goat. It was not grazing, but stood
stock still staring at the jungle. From time to time it
uttered a nervous little bleat. Did it know its
danger? James wondered, feeling sorry for the poor,
lonely little beast. He was sorry this was necessary.

Time passed. Without any distraction it seemed
to be standing still. The cloud still hung like a
black curtain over the moon. At intervals the goat
whimpered its pathetic little cry. Fear was in the
air. James could feel it in the beating of his heart.
He felt safe in the *machan* but the knowledge that
somewhere in the pool of darkness below the killer
might be stalking its prey caused his nerves to
tingle and his lips to dry.

Then came the rain. Not a deluge. Not even a
storm. Just big scattered drops that pattered on the
broad-leafed evergreen foliage making a sound like
approaching footsteps. James understood what the
Skipper had said about rain spoiling the plan. He
looked at him expecting him to say something:
but he did not speak. He did not move. He had
slumped into a most uncomfortable position with
his head between his knees. The rifle had fallen
across his feet. James peered at him. Could he
have fallen asleep? He seemed to be in some danger
of falling off the *machan*. "Are you all right,
Skipper?" he whispered.

No answer.

James touched him gently on the arm, suddenly assailed by a feeling that something was wrong. "What's the matter, Skipper?"

The answer was a groan of agony.

"What is it, sir?"

The Skipper seemed to fight for breath. He groaned again. "It's—another—heart—attack."

"The pills," James said, remembering what had been said in the bungalow. "Where are the pills?"

"I left them—in—the haversack." The words ended in a spasm.

"The haversack!" James' own heart seemed to die in him as he remembered the haversack had been left in the headman's house. His brain whirled. Without the pills . . . by daylight it might be too late. He could not sit there and watch his companion die. His brain cleared suddenly as he perceived there was only one thing for it. The pills would have to be fetched. He looked down. Somewhere in the blackness below the goat bleated dismally. There was a new note in its voice. Terror. The steady patter of raindrops drowned all other sounds.

Now he knew what he had to do James did not hesitate. First he took off the long muffler that he had really worn as a protection against mosquitoes and tied the Skipper's arm to a branch so that he could not fall off the *machan*. He picked up the torch and directed the beam into the clearing. But the beam was weak and did not reach far. All he could see was the goat. It was standing rigid, staring at a certain point of the jungle. He flicked off the torch and put it in his pocket. Then, cold with such a fear as he had never known, he went down the steps. On the ground, torch in hand, he set off up the track that led to the village.

Then followed a nightmare never to be forgotten. To make matters worse, the light of the torch dropped to a glimmer, its battery apparently exhausted. James walked on at a steady pace. Only by an effort did he refrain from breaking into a run which he knew would end in panic-stricken flight. His only hope, he told himself, was to keep his head. The raindrops splashed, every drop a stealthy rustle, a footstep in the jungle.

The village came into sight. Some of the houses showed lights. Every door was shut, as he expected. He reached the first. A low murmur of voices came from inside. He knocked. The voices stopped. He could hear no movement. He banged on the door. "Let me in," he shouted, feeling his nerve failing. The door remained closed. Even at that terrible moment he could not blame the fear-petrified people inside.

He walked on to the next door. The same thing happened. It took another effort to walk the fifty yards to the headman's house. A light showed at the window but the door of course was shut and bolted. He hammered on it, shouting "Open". No answer. "Open the door, it's me." No answer. His voice rose. "Shall I tell the world that Hamid Lal with a medal has the liver of a chicken?" he

yelled desperately. A pause. A bolt was drawn.
The door opened an inch. James thrust it wide and
rushed in. Even before he could turn he heard the
door slammed and bolted. Hamid Lal stared at
him, eyes saucering with dismay. He seemed incapable of speech.

"Lovell *sahib* is sick," informed James curtly.
"He must have medicine. It's in here." He
picked up the haversack and turned out the contents. Another moment and the little bottle of pills
was in his pocket. "I need a torch," he went on
tersely. Hamid Lal pointed to a number that
leaned against the wall; short sticks with a bundle
of dry grass and brushwood tied to the end. James
snatched one and lit it at the little open fire burning
on the hearth. "Now let me out," he ordered.

"No."

"*Open the door!*"

"No, *sahib*."

James thrust the old man aside, marvelling that
a man of known courage could be reduced to such
terror by superstition. Opening the door, holding
the torch high he strode out into the deserted
village. Instantly the door was slammed and
bolted behind him. An awful feeling of loneliness
swept over him and he had to brace himself not to
rush back into the house. Instead, with calculated
deliberation, his teeth set, he marched back down
the track towards the *machan*. The thought did not
occur to him but never in his life would he be
confronted with such a test as the one to which he

set his face as he set off down that dreadful track aware of what might be waiting. His every nerve screamed at him to go back.

Half-way to the *machan* the moon came out from behind the cloud and everything was bathed in an eerie blue light that only made the shadows under the trees the more impenetrable. The rain stopped but water still dripped from the leaves with sounds like breathing, furtive movements . . .

The clearing came into sight. James' every instinct was to turn and rush away from the fearful place. Stone cold, dry-lipped, he went on without altering his pace. The goat was still there. It was not grazing. It made no sound. Quivering in every limb it stared fixedly at something on the edge of the clearing. At what? What could it see? James had a grim suspicion. As he drew near a wave of intense sympathy for the poor little beast, tethered and unable to escape, surged over him. With it came a sudden fury; a burning hatred of the tiger. With a wild yell he dashed forward and hurled the blazing torch at the spot where the goat was staring. He did not wait to see the result. He made for the tree and went up the ladder like a monkey. As he mounted two significant sounds followed him. One was a deep-throated *woof* that was certainly not made by the goat. The other was a crash of brushwood.

Panting, he fell on the platform. The Skipper was still there just as he had left him; hunched up, moaning feebly. James took out the bottle of pills.

His hands were so shaky that he nearly dropped them. He unscrewed the cap of the water-bottle and raising the half-conscious man by the shoulder held it to his mouth, in his haste spilling some of the contents. "Drink," he pleaded hoarsely. "Come on, Skipper. Drink. Try. I've got the pills."

The Skipper's eyes opened, dull, unseeing. James parted his lips and slipped a pill in his mouth. "Drink," he ordered firmly. The Skipper took a sip and swallowed.

"Got it?"

"Yes."

"Good. Drink some more water to make sure."

The sick man made the effort and then fell back breathing heavily. Two or three minutes passed. Then he said weakly: "Ah! Thanks. That's better."

"Have another pill?"

"Not now. Later."

James snatched a glance down into the moonlit glade. The goat was still there. Nibbling grass. The torch had burned itself out. He untied the securing muffler.

Presently the Skipper raised himself into a sitting position. In a curious voice, as if the thought had just struck him, he said: "The pills. Where were they?"

"In your haversack."

"How did they get here?"

"I fetched them."

A pause, as if the meaning of this was sinking

home. "Do you mean—you've been—to the village?" asked the Skipper incredulously.

"Of course."

"Oh my God!" murmured Captain Lovell. "If your father ever learns I let you do that he'll shoot me."

"You didn't let me," corrected James cheerfully. "You didn't know anything about it. I shan't tell him if you don't."

"Did you see the tiger?"

"No, but he was there. I shooed him off by throwing a torch at him."

The Skipper made a queer noise in his throat. "So you shooed off a man-eater, eh!" A little later, in a voice that was fast gathering strength, he went on. "Let me tell you something, James. If you live to be a hundred you'll never do a braver thing than what you did tonight—and I know what I'm talking about. I don't regard myself as a coward, but I wouldn't have gone down those steps for all the treasures in India. Not even with a rifle."

"What else would you expect me to do?" protested James. "Now let me tell *you* something. If I'm ever more frightened than I was this night I doubt if I'd live to tell the tale. I was petrified. When your torch packed up on me I really thought I'd die."

"That's the real test of courage, James," said the Skipper seriously. "It's easy for a man who doesn't know the meaning of fear to be brave. It's the man who *is* afraid, but faces up to it, who deserves a royal salute. Such men are gold. Pure gold. Now tell me what happened."

James told him.

They sat on the *machan* till dawn without seeing or hearing anything of the tiger. "You scared him," said the Skipper as, taking the goat with them they returned to the village. "Not many men can say they've scared a man-eater."

And it may be said here that the tiger never again troubled the village of Cungit. Hamid Lal may have been right when he explained, simply: "His demon warned him to go away, for here death awaited him."

For some time after this adventure three words spoken by Captain Lovell remained in James' memory. They were 'Gold. Pure gold.' Had he, he wondered, established a false reputation, one that might be difficult to live up to? Had he, like a soldier who wins the Victoria Cross, set a standard for courage that would have to be maintained or invite criticism? We on our part may wonder how far this affected his future career.

A CHAPTER OF ADVENTURES

It started when a runner arrived breathless from Bandali, a village some six or seven miles up in the foothills north of the bungalow where resided the Assistant Commissioner of the United Provinces in India, Bigglesworth *sahib*, when he had business in that part of his district. The gist of the message the man brought was this.

A Forest Survey officer named Mr. Lane had arrived at the village following complaints that a leopard was causing trouble, killing cattle and goats. This leopard had become bold and had often been seen. It was old and had lost an eye; but it was cunning. It had been wounded and was now doubly dangerous. It had made its lair in an area of *lantana* (a creeping shrub that forms dense thickets) close to the village. As this would be too dangerous to enter on foot Mr. Lane had sent for an elephant hoping to get a shot from its back, which would command a wide view. He found he was short of cartridges for his rifle, a .476 Westley Richards, so could the Assistant Commissioner please send him up a packet by the messenger.

This was a simple request and not an unusual one. But it so happened that the man to whom it was addressed was ill with an attack of dysentery, and the message was actually taken by one of the office staff, Lalu Din. With him at the time was his son, Habu, a lad of fourteen, and the Commissioner's twelve-year-old son, James. They had been talking in the garden when the weary messenger arrived, and suspecting something was wrong had followed him in. James at once took the message to his father, whose answer was:

"Send him the cartridges. You'll find some in the magazine."

"Shall I take them myself?" asked James.

"Why?"

"The messenger is exhausted. He has run all the way. He needs a rest. I have been to Bandali two or three times so I know the way."

The sick man hesitated.

"It's perfectly safe," prompted James. "There's a track all the way. Habu can come with me for company. We'll be back before sunset and perhaps be able to tell you the leopard has been shot."

"Very well. But keep out of the way. Hunting a wounded leopard is no business for boys. And come back before dark. You know the night air is bad for you."

"I'll stay in the village while Mr. Lane does the hunting and then come straight back," promised James. "I'll get the cartridges." Well satisfied he went to the magazine where the cartridges were kept, put a packet in his pocket and rejoined Lalu Din who was giving the messenger some refreshment. "I'm taking the cartridges myself," he announced.

"This man needs a rest. May Habu come with me to keep me company?"

Lalu Din raised no objection. It was no great distance to the village where Mr. Lane was waiting. There was a forest path all the way, part of it through tea estates where men and women would be working, so there was no danger—or so it could be assumed.

In a few minutes the boys were on their way, James wearing shirt, shorts, light shoes and sun helmet, Habu merely a loin cloth. Neither carried a weapon, partly to save weight and because it was not supposed that one would be needed. James meant every word he had said to his father. Certainly he had not the slightest intention of going anywhere near a wounded leopard.

Travelling non-stop they made good time.

A mile short of the objective they came to a bridge. They knew it was there. James had crossed it more than once and had taken it for granted that it was safe, although to anyone unaccustomed to native bridges the crossing might be an alarming experience. This one was a particularly primitive affair. Four hand-made grass ropes had been thrown across a precipitous-sided *nullah* perhaps thirty yards wide. The ropes were braced together at intervals. Across the lower pair some slats had been tied to form a sort of catwalk for pedestrians only. A hundred feet below a torrent of muddy water foamed its way through a chaos of fallen rocks.

B

The trouble with these home-made bridges—if one can call them that—is this. Once erected it is nobody's business to do anything to them. They are expected to last for ever. In fact, they last only until they break, when some unlucky traveller comes to grief. Naturally, not an uncommon occurrence.

No such thought entered James' head. It is better not to think about such things. He sat down to wipe the sweat from his face with his handkerchief, for the air was hot and sticky, with the result that Habu went on to make the crossing first. As James watched him, without any particular interest, it suddenly struck him that the flimsy structure was sagging and swaying more than it should. However, perhaps this was because Habu was striding along in the manner of one who has done this sort of thing all his life and thinks nothing of it.

He was about half-way across, with James just starting to follow, when it happened. There came a soft twang. The bridge dropped in the middle, some five or six feet. Some slats hurtled down into the torrent. More dangled, end on. Another rope snapped. Part of the bridge, with Habu clinging to it, hung suspended over the chasm.

At the first lurch James thought the entire bridge had gone. He clutched at one of the two hand ropes. It remained secure. From this position he saw his companion swinging like a pendulum on a single rope from what remained of the middle of the bridge. "Hang on, Habu," he yelled, although it was hard to see what he could do. Common sense urged him to get back to the bank he had just left while it was still possible. "Hold on," he shouted again, his racing brain telling him that should he add his weight to that of his Indian friend at the weakest part of the bridge the whole thing would collapse and they would both fall to their deaths in the raging flood below. But to leave Habu in that awful position, absolutely helpless, was unthinkable.

Hardly knowing what he was doing, for his actions were no longer the result of serious thought, hand over hand he went on along the hand ropes. The bridge lurched. It sagged sickeningly. The flimsy structure creaked. More slats fell. Every second, it seemed, must be the last. Then, suddenly, fear vanished. Stone cold, he was concerned only with what he was doing, or attempting to do.

Unbelievably the remaining ropes held and he reached the lowest part, which was of course immediately above Habu. But he was still out of reach: by at least three feet. James considered the situation. Part of the broken bridge to which he was clinging was a trifle lower. Low enough for him to be able to touch Habu. Even if he went down, should the bridge hold, which seemed unlikely, he doubted if he would have the strength to pull his friend up.

"I can't hold on much longer," cried Habu desperately.

"Wait! I'm coming," encouraged James, and

began to lower himself down the tangle of ropes, bamboo, and slats. This, although terrifying, helped him when it sagged lower under his weight and he found himself nearly alongside his friend. With all his weight on his arms his own strength was fast failing. He realized that to pull Habu up was out of the question. "Habu," he said through his teeth. "Do you hear me?" He was not sure because of the noise made by the rushing water.

"Yes."

"Get hold of my legs and climb up to the rope."

"I can't."

"You must. It's the only way. Try."

James felt Habu's arms close over his legs in a grip of iron. Slowly, inch by inch, the Indian began to drag his slim body up his own. The bridge creaked horribly. It seemed impossible that it could bear the double weight. James flinched as Habu's finger nails clawed into the skin of his neck. There was a dreadful moment when his shirt began to tear, but the collar held, choking him. Then, suddenly, the strain ended, and he realized that Habu had reached the hand rope. He expected him to go on to safety. He hoped he would, to shift some of the weight from what was obviously the weakest part of what remained of the bridge. Instead, looking up, he saw him lying flat on some slats offering his hands.

"Go," choked James.

"Come," cried Habu.

James thought it no time to argue. Exerting his

last ounce of strength he took the hands and in a moment lay gasping beside his companion. "Go," he panted, too exhausted himself to move.

Habu crawled along the slanting slats that still held and reached the far bank. After a pause to get his breath James followed him and collapsed in a bank of ferns gasping like a stranded fish. For a little while neither spoke. Then they met each other's eyes and Habu managed to force a sickly smile.

James, who saw nothing funny in what had happened, voiced the first question that came into his head. "How are we going to get home?"

"There will be other ways across the river," declared Habu confidently. "Someone from the village will show us the way they used before there was a bridge."

"I hope you are right," James said. "Let's go on. Mr. Lane will be waiting for the cartridges." He felt in his pocket to make sure they were still there after his exertions.

Rising, they went on their way.

MORE TROUBLE

THE boys might be pardoned for thinking they had had enough adventure for one day, had they thought about it. There were no more bridges to cross, anyway. But if this was what they hoped they were mistaken. The real problem, although they were unaware of it, was not behind them but in front. The first indication of this came when, on the jungle-lined track leading into the village, from somewhere ahead came a gunshot. A minute or two later there was an outcry of cries and screams mingled with the trumpeting of an elephant.

The boys stopped. They looked at each other.

"Something happens," said Habu.

Before James could point out that this was evident, down the track came rushing a man wild-eyed and obviously terrified. He did not stop, and such was his haste that he nearly knocked them over. He shouted something, but what it was James did not catch. Naturally, he thought it had something to do with the leopard, and looked quickly for a handy tree to climb. "What's the matter with him? What did he say?" he asked Habu.

"He said elephant."

"Mr. Lane's elephant, perhaps."

"Yes."

"That would be a trained elephant."

Habu shrugged.

"We'd better find out what's going on."

They had not gone far when another distraught man came racing down the track. He, too, would have passed, but James caught him by the arm and held him. "What is it?" he asked in Hindi.

The man broke into an incoherent babble too fast for him to follow. Habu understood, and when the man broke off he explained.

The man with them had seen the leopard sunning itself on the edge of the *lantana* near its lair. He had told Mr. Lane who, thinking this was an opportunity not to be missed had decided not to wait for the extra cartridges. He had gone on the elephant, with its regular *mahout*. (Elephant keeper and driver.) The man with them, who had seen the leopard, had also gone on the elephant to mark its position. The leopard was still there. Mr. Lane had shot at it but only wounded it. Whereupon the leopard had charged. It had jumped on the elephant's trunk to get at the men on its back. The elephant, mad with fear and pain, had stampeded, throwing its head about to dislodge the creature that had its claws in its trunk. Mr. Lane had been thrown off, dropping his rifle. Then the *mahout* fell. The elephant had trampled him to death. It then rushed towards the village, throwing off the leopard on the way. The man with them, seeing his chance, had jumped off and was running for his life when

he met them. The elephant, in a frenzy, was
running wild, beserk.

"Where is it now?" James asked the man.

He answered it was in the village smashing everything it could reach.

"Where is Mr. Lane?"

The man didn't know. The last he had seen of
him was when he had been thrown off the elephant.

"I think we will go back," Habu said sensibly.

"Go back if you wish. I shall go on," replied
James in a matter-of-fact voice; which did not mean
he under-estimated the risks. To take on a wounded
leopard, unarmed, with a fear-crazed elephant into
the bargain, seemed little short of lunacy; but the
appalling predicament of Mr. Lane could not be
ignored. He might be dead. On the other hand he
might still be alive and helpless. Things couldn't be
left like that. Something would have to be done.
Just what James did not know. All he knew was he
would have to do something—or at least try.

"I will see what the elephant is doing," he said,
and walked on up the path.

Habu followed. A little way behind him came the
village man. Clearly, he did not like this idea at all,
and it is to his credit that he stayed with them.
There was no more shouting in the village but
there were other more ominous sounds.

When the jungle opened out to allow the village
to come into view the situation was instantly
apparent. Not a soul was in sight. But there stood
the elephant, with blood streaming down its trunk,

looking around suspiciously. It squealed, and trotting over to a house that stood on stilts proceeded to demolish it, tearing up the corner posts and flinging them aside in a paroxysm of fury. It was plain that in this state it was unapproachable.

James turned to the villager. "Where did the accident happen?"

The man pointed to a broad track that ended in a field of tussocky grass.

"How far?"

"Close."

"Wait here," James said.

"I will come with you," Habu said.

"Wait," ordered James sternly. "One is enough."

With the caution the situation demanded, taking care not to make a noise or show himself, he began picking a way through the jungle to get nearer to the field. He had not far to go. The first thing he saw when he reached the rough grass was the almost naked body of a brown man, evidently the unfortunate *mahout*. It did not move. He crept on. Presently he made out the spots of the leopard; lying still, stretched out in the grass. James watched it intently for a minute. Was it dead? A swarm of flies over it suggested it might be. How to make sure? He marked an escape route up a tree, picked up a piece of dead wood and threw it. It didn't hit the leopard but it fell near. The beast did not move.

He went on a little way, eyes seeking what he most anxiously sought. Mr. Lane. If the leopard had killed him, or mauled him, he should not be far away. He could not see him. Climbing on the low-hanging branch of a tree he surveyed the scene of the tragedy. He dare not call for fear the leopard was still alive. A white object half buried in a tuft of grass caught his eye. He made it out to be a sun helmet. Nearby, a long object could just be seen in some longer grass. The light clothes worn by a white man? If so it could only be Mr. Lane.

With the leopard so near it took all James' nerve to break cover, but having done so he walked quickly towards the spot. On the way he picked up a rifle. A .476 Westley Richards. The safety catch was off. He jerked open the breech. An expended cartridge fell out. He reloaded quickly from the ammunition he had brought with him. Feeling better with a weapon in his hands, keeping a wary eye on the leopard he hurried on. He saw the object was the hunter. Even before he reached him he thought from the absence of bloodstains on his clothes he had not been mauled.

Coming up he saw his eyes were open. He knelt beside him.

"Where are you hurt?" he asked quickly.

Mr. Lane's eyes opened wider. "Young Bigglesworth, isn't it?"

"Yes. Never mind that. I——"

"Watch out. There's a wounded leopard——"

"I've seen it. I think it's dead. Can you walk?"

"No. I think my leg's broken. Elephant stepped on it. Can't move my shoulder. I landed on it when I fell. Broken something there, too."

"I can't carry you so I shall have to leave you while I fetch help," said James tersely. "I'll be as quick as I can. First I'll make sure the leopard is dead."

"Where's the elephant?"

"In the village. It's mad. I shall have to shoot it or I shan't be able to get helpers." With that James hurried off.

First he went to the leopard, finger on trigger ready to shoot at the first sign of movement. It was dead, with a pool of blood under its mouth. Mightily relieved he walked on quickly to the *mahout*. To his amazement, on his arrival the man sat up.

"They told me you were dead," blurted James.

"Not dead, *sahib*."

"I can see that," retorted James sarcastically. "They said the elephant trod on you."

"No. I hold her leg."

Just what the man meant by this James did not waste time to inquire. "Why did you stay here?" he asked, puzzled.

"Stay still. Then leopard think I'm dead."

"It's dead," informed James. "Can you walk?"

The man stood up and put the matter to test and found that he could, if somewhat stiffly.

"Come with me," ordered James, and carried on towards the village.

The *mahout* followed.

Coming in sight of the houses they saw the elephant was still there: standing still by the demolished hut on which apparently it had worked

off its rage. It looked more normal, but James
thought it would be unwise to trust it. He wanted
helpers to carry the stricken hunter. "I shall have to
shoot it," he decided.

"No, *sahib*. No shoot," the *mahout* pleaded. "Good
elephant. My friend." And with that he started
walking towards the animal making coaxing noises
and calling "Fatima, Fatima," presumably the
elephant's name.

Either it understood or recognized its master's
voice, for the effect was electrical. The elephant
spun round in its own length. For an instant it
stared. It uttered a whimpering little cry and with
its trunk held high trotted towards them.

James, anything but happy, held his fire, still
prepared for trouble. But his fears were soon dis-
pelled, and presently he was staring incredulously
at the astonishing spectacle of the *mahout*, with tears
running down his face, caressing the big beast's
injured trunk as it was held out to him as if for
sympathy. From the queer noises it made the
elephant might have been weeping, too.

Touching though it was, James had too much
to do than allow this to go on. "You'd better do
something; wash the blood off," he advised. "There
should be some disinfectant in Mr. Lane's luggage."

The *mahout*, with a hand on the elephant's trunk,
walked off.

Habu must have seen all this, for he now came
running. In fact, now the danger was past people
appeared from all directions. James was thinking

quickly; and it may be remarked here that it was this early training that taught him to make quick decisions; and act on them.

"The leopard is dead. Mr. Lane has been hurt," he told Habu swiftly. "He needs a doctor. Find a man who knows the way to the Forest Post where he is stationed. There should be a doctor there."

Such a man was found. In fact, two. They went off together at a run.

"Now we shall have to see about getting Mr. Lane into the village," went on James tersely. "He can't walk. Get some men to cut bamboos to make a frame for a stretcher. I'll leave that to you. I must go back to Mr. Lane. Bring the stretcher along as soon as it's ready. It isn't far to go." He hurried back to the injured man, and to make the story short, in less than half-an-hour Mr. Lane had been brought in and made as comfortable as possible on the floor of the headman's house. He was in some pain, but he assured James there was nothing more he could do. The doctor would do whatever was necessary.

James was relieved to hear this. The sun was already getting low, and as he told Habu, they had better be on their way or their fathers would be getting anxious. A guide was found who knew a way to cross the river without using the bridge and they set off.

The crossing proved to be a final test of nerve. It involved the descent of an almost sheer cliff to the water. The only way of getting to the other side of the raging water was by stepping, and sometimes jumping, from rock to rock. Being wet with spray they were slippery, and a fall could have been fatal. There was a stiff climb up the opposite bank to reach the level ground above, then a long walk through thick jungle to reach the track where it ended at the collapsed bridge. However, all this was accomplished without accident.

With night fast falling the boys hurried on towards home, some time later to meet a party led by Lalu Din, Habu's father, that had been sent out to look for them. There had been anxiety on their account.

Tired, and more than a little leg-weary, James arrived home in moonlight and went at once to see his father to explain his delayed return. He had to describe in detail all that had happened.

Said his father, seriously, shaking his head: "I'm afraid, James, you're taking too much on yourself."

"What else could I do?" protested James.

"Keep away from trouble, or one of these days you'll end up badly. It won't be for much longer. You'll soon be on your way to England. There you will have fewer opportunities to take risks, at all events with dangerous animals. Now you'd better have something to eat and get to bed, or we'll be having you down with another relapse of fever."

"Yes, sir," replied James obediently.

DEATH IN THE WATER

THE crocodile occurs in all warm-water countries, in rivers, lakes, and sometimes in the sea off the coast, notably in the vicinity of islands. By any standards it is a loathsome beast. With age it can grow to an enormous size. It is a flesh eater. Year after year it takes a steady toll of life, both animal and human, for which reason it is hated and feared by everyone. Samuel Baker, the celebrated explorer and big game hunter, and a man not given to exaggeration, tells of seeing crocodiles with the girth of a hippopotamus.

Even the largest mammals, except perhaps the elephant, can fall victim to its voracious appetite. Some years ago an explorer named Max Fleischman secured a remarkable series of photographs, which caused a sensation at the time, of a crocodile killing a rhinoceros. It was dragged into the water and drowned. When one considers the size, weight and power of a rhinoceros, it is easy to realize what little hope a man would have once those terrible jaws had closed on him. Hunters who would face a charging lion "without turning a hair" have been known to blanch at the idea of being seized by a crocodile. There is probably no more terrible death.

There are crocodiles in all the rivers of India. Everyone in the country knows that. Boys know it as a European boy learns that wasps have stings. Young James Bigglesworth knew a lot about these beasts, mostly from hearsay, because he took no chances of meeting one and therefore seldom saw one of man-eating size. There were occasionally fatal accidents. These occurred most commonly among women who went to the river to fetch water or to wash their clothes. Crocodiles know these places, and when one of the brutes is known to have taken up residence it makes life difficult for the people who have to rely on the river for water.

It was almost inevitable that sooner or later James would encounter one. This is how it came about. There was a river, not a very big one, about a quarter of a mile from the village. It was, as a matter of detail, the same river that he had crossed with Habu to reach Bandali, when the bridge had broken as described in an earlier chapter. But that was much higher up, where the water, icy cold, made its first rush down the hills from the snow-covered mountains. There it was too cold and too fast to attract crocodiles. But by the time it had reached the lower ground it had warmed up and for the most part took a more sluggish course, occasional rocky rushes linking deep, quiet pools. Its course lay through jungle, trees and scrub pressing along its banks, sometimes overhanging to make a near approach difficult.

One day, James, out for a stroll, for no particular

reason took a path that ended at the river. This path had been made by generations of women walking from the village to the river for the purposes described earlier. There was a reason why the path ran in this particular direction. It had its terminus at one of the few open places on the bank of the river. This was a small stony beach caused by the water swinging round a bend. For the same reason it had formed a wide deep pool, shallow on the near side but running deep under the opposite bank. Towards one end of the beach, half in the water, was a great sloping slab of black rock which must have been cast there in ages past by a particularly heavy spate. The upper surface of this rock had been worn smooth as polished marble by countless women beating their wet clothes on it to clean them, as is the customary manner in India. The reason why the place was known in the village as the Black Rock was obvious.

James reached the spot to find it occupied by three small boys, aged about seven, who were disporting themselves in the shallow water, splashing each other and making a lot of noise, as boys will. They may not have been able to swim. At all events, fortunately for them, they did not go in above their waists. This could not have been for fear of crocodiles because the pool had the reputation of being safe. At any rate, there had never been any trouble there.

James, hot and a little leg-weary, sat down to rest before starting on the walk home. He did not

go down to the beach but took up a position a little
to one side where the water flowed round a low but
rather steep grassy bank. He was himself tempted
to have a "dip" but refrained because, being hot,
he was afraid of taking a chill.

He had been sitting there for some minutes,
amused by the boys' antics, when he noticed a
ripple on the deeper water farther out in the stream.
Being of a curious nature he watched it, thinking
perhaps it was a *mahseer*, a fish rather like a salmon
which can run up to a fair size. It is common in
many Indian rivers. He began to have second
thoughts when the ripple took on a definite V
shape and began to move faster towards the place
where the boys were playing. Then, when two
knobs appeared above the surface just beyond the
point of the ripple he realized the truth. They were
the eyes of a crocodile, and a large one.

With a yell of warning he sprang to his feet. The
boys, sensing danger, made for the beach. Quick
though James had been he was not fast enough.
Two of the boys splashed their way on to the
stones. The other, who had been almost below him,
had farther to go. The water being clear James
could now see the dark shape streaking through the
water like a great arrow. This last boy just failed
to reach the bank. He let out a scream of terror,
and after clutching wildly at the air stumbled and
fell. Through the turmoil in the water James saw
the crocodile had him by the leg. The other two
boys, seeing what had happened, danced about

helplessly, waving their arms and screaming—which in fact was about all they could do.

James, on his feet, looked down in horror. There was apparently nothing he could do, either. He had no weapon, merely a light walking cane, and that was useless for such an occasion. As he stared the crocodile's head showed above the surface of the water. Hardly knowing what he was doing, but seized with a burning hatred of the reptile, he braced himself and jumped. His heels landed squarely on the hideous head. The shock of this must have caused the crocodile to release its hold on the boy. James, of course, unable to keep his balance, fell. That was almost inevitable. But he was on his feet in an instant. Grabbing the madly struggling boy by the hair he somehow managed to drag him to the beach, and safety. Where the reptile went he didn't know. He didn't see it again. Not that he spent much time looking for it. Shaking, and stone cold with fear when he realized what he had done, James gave himself a moment to recover and then turned his attention to the boy, now lying on the beach groaning and crying with one of his legs fairly spurting blood. The other two boys just stood staring, wild-eyed, mouths open but dumb with shock.

James tried to stop the blood with his handkerchief but couldn't make much of a job of it. What with the boy kicking and blood and water all over the place he couldn't really see what he was doing. Shouting to the uninjured boys to hold their friend he took off the pith helmet he was wearing and ripping off the *puggaree* used that for a bandage, twisting the ends into a tourniquet with his cane, which, curiously enough, he still held. This done he hesitated, uncertain of what to do next. After all he himself was agitated by what had happened, and the speed of it. His first-aid was only a temporary measure, and certainly anything but professional; but then, he was wet, his patient was wet, and the mixture of water and blood made things difficult.

With an effort he got control of himself and did some quick thinking. In the state the injured boy was in there could be no question of him walking home, presumably to the village. Nor could he, even with the help of his two companions, carry him. He could see only one thing for it. In any case there was no resident doctor in the village. He realized the boy's wounds needed drastic treatment if they were not to turn septic. He had been told more than once that people who had been mauled by tooth or claw died more often from the wounds turning septic than from the wounds themselves.

Automatically he took command. First the injured boy was moved to a safe place well clear of the river. Then, telling the others to stay with him, and not allow him to move, he set off for home at a run. He ran all the way. Arriving, without stopping for explanations, he dashed to the medicine chest, took lint, a roll of bandages and a bottle of antiseptic liquid kept for emergencies. With these in his hand he ran back to the river to find four women, with bundles of clothes for washing, now on the scene. He warned them of the danger in the river and then set to work on the injured boy, now only half conscious from delayed shock.

He screamed with pain as James poured antiseptic into the tooth holes and lacerations. James knew the stuff would sting, but he ordered the women to hold the boy still and went on with his life-saving operation. By the time he had finished two men, who had heard the screaming and had come to see what it was about, were there.

"Does anyone know where this boy lives?" asked James, standing up.

The women said they knew, whereupon James ordered them to act as guides while the two men carried the boy home. "Tell his mother to put him to bed and keep him there," he said. "He should be all right now."

The entire party of natives, men, women and boys, moved off. James watched them go, and then sat down for a minute or two to recover from his exertions. He himself was feeling the strain of the last hectic half hour. Having rested he too set off for home, wet, dishevelled and smeared with bloodstains. He would have changed his clothes before seeing his father, but he found his father waiting, rumours having already reached him.

His father did not waste time scolding. He looked hard at James, and seeing the state he was in simply said "Well?"—a question that called for an explanation.

"I'm all right, sir," said James.

"What happened?"

James explained, briefly.

When he had finished his father was staring incredulously. "Are you saying you jumped on the head of the crocodile?"

"Yes, sir."

"You must have been raving mad."

"I think I must have been," admitted James. "But something had to be done. What else could I do?"

"Yes, I can see it was difficult," conceded his father. "But you'd better go and get changed. Then I'll see you in my study."

"Yes, sir." James went off.

Twenty minutes later the conversation was resumed in the study. Lalu Din, one of the office staff, was there.

"Where did this happen?" James was asked.

"At the Black Rock pool."

"I've never heard of a dangerous crocodile there."

"Well, I can assure you there's one there now."

Lalu Din spoke. "It must have come up the river from Baradad, *sahib*. I heard there was one there. He has taken several women, so they say."

"See that all the women in the village are warned not to go near the Black Rock."

"I fancy the word will have gone round already," James said. "This is going to make things difficult for them. It is the only place where there is easy access to the water."

"Well, I don't see what we can do about it."

"Surely there's one thing we could do, sir."

"Indeed? What's that?"

"Make life too uncomfortable for the crocodile to stay in the pool."

"How would you propose to do that?"

"By sitting on the bank and shooting at him every time he shows himself."

"And who's going to sit all day on the bank, watching?"

"I could do that."

"*You!*"

Lalu Din smiled at this.

"Why not? It needn't interfere with my lessons. I could take one of my books with me," James said.

It should be explained that at this time James was studying at home, no day school being available and his indifferent health making boarding-school impracticable.

His father considered the proposal dubiously.

"I couldn't take any harm," urged James. "Obviously I wouldn't be such a fool as to go in the water. Something will have to be done. Whatever you say the women will still go to the Black Rock, as they always have. You know that. Sooner or later one will be taken."

This was an argument his father could not dispute, as James well knew.

"Very well," was the decision. "I'll allow you to take your rifle to the pool if you'll give me your word that under no conditions will you set foot in the water."

"You have my most solemn word for that, sir," declared James. And he meant it.

That ended the conversation.

The following morning saw James early at the pool. He found the place deserted. There was not a soul there. Obviously word of the accident had gone round. James approached quietly and cautiously. He found a seat on the bank, where he had sat the previous day, and surveyed the dark water. There was not a sign of the crocodile. In fact there was not a sign of any living creature. But he did not allow himself to be deceived. He knew the crocodile would be there, somewhere. Where he may have made a mistake was to suppose that the crocodile would be unable to leave its lair, probably under the far bank where the water ran deep, without him seeing it. Again, he knew the crocodile to be a beast of low intelligence, but he had yet to learn that such creatures are usually compensated by being endowed with an acute form of cunning. If that were not so they would not be able to live.

Time went on. James had brought a book but he did not read. He was too engrossed in what he was doing. His rifle, loaded, lay across his knees, the safety catch off. All he wanted was a glimpse of the crocodile so that he could use it. In his dealings with nature he tried to be fair, but for a man-killing crocodile he felt nothing but loathing and hatred.

Patiently he waited for an opportunity to express how he felt.

This was to come sooner than he expected, but certainly not in the manner he had confidently anticipated. Naturally, he supposed that if the beast showed itself it would be in the river. But in the event things did not work out like that. The mounting heat of the sun tended to make him drowsy, but he remained on the alert determined not to miss a chance. It was as well that he did.

A slight sound behind him, like the soft crushing of twigs, made him turn his head to ascertain the cause. Instead of seeing one of the village women as he expected he found himself staring into the face of the crocodile from a distance of two or three yards. Standing erect on its legs, with its back arched it looked like a prehistoric monster. Its jaws were agape, revealing rows of filthy teeth. Seeing that it had been observed—and all wild animals seem to have this faculty—it rushed at him.

James had no time to move, to get up. All he could do, still in the sitting position, was swing his rifle round, and without bringing it to his shoulder, with the muzzle practically in the beast's open mouth, pull the trigger. Almost simultaneously he scrambled to his feet, only to have his legs swept from under him by the creature's heavy tail, which flashed round in the manner these reptiles commonly employ to knock a victim, man or beast, into the water. James was knocked clean into the river. Even while falling the thought in his mind was, "I mustn't drop the rifle."

He held on to it. Fortunately the water was shallow, so he was on his feet in an instant, splashing his way to the stones of the beach. He did not stop to look round to see what the crocodile was doing. Not until he was on dry land did he do that, jerking a fresh cartridge into the breech of his rifle at the same time.

The crocodile, coughing blood, had not moved. Its eyes glared. But it was far from dead. It rose up and made another rush. James dashed up the beach to get well away from the water. The crocodile did not follow him but stumbled on to the edge of the river where it lay, still coughing horribly, half in and half out of the water.

Breathless from shock and excitement James steadied himself. Then he took careful aim at the beast's head and fired. At the impact of the bullet the crocodile went flat on its stomach and tried to drag itself into the water. Now, feeling secure, James advanced a few paces and put another bullet behind the shoulder; and he continued to pump bullets into the creature while there was a cartridge left in the magazine. By the time he had finished the great lizard was no longer moving. Blood from its mouth was staining the water crimson. James reloaded and stood ready to shoot again should it show signs of life. A minute passed. It did not move.

Voices on the bank above caused him to snatch a

glance and he saw he had an audience. Two women had arrived with their bundles of washing. They called something to him, but he was too taken up with watching the crocodile to catch what they said. Only when he was satisfied that it was really dead did he wring the water from his hair and look for his helmet, which had fallen off. He saw it floating down the river. He did not trouble to go after it. In fact, he couldn't, for now that the peril had passed reaction set in and his legs felt so weak that he had to sit down. He was trembling from shock.

The women, talking excitedly, came forward to look at the crocodile and heap praises on him, calling him "heaven-sent", and similar compliments. Presently Lalu Din ran up, saying that the shooting had been heard in the village and he had been sent to find out what had happened.

James simply pointed at the crocodile.

When Lalu Din saw it he threw up his hands and turned his eyes to heaven. "But you are wet, *sahib*. You have been in the river," he accused. "You promised . . ."

"I didn't go in," broke in James. "I was knocked in. It came at me from behind."

"Ah! The devil was in him."

"Well, now he's got some bullets in him as well. If anyone wants a crocodile he can have this one. I'm going home."

On his way James realized how narrow had been his escape. He had assumed the crocodile would be in the river. He now perceived that while he had been stalking it, it had been stalking him. There was an obvious lesson in that. Never to take anything for granted.

Some days later, when he had related the incident to his *shikari* friend, Captain Lovell, another lesson was pointed out to him. With a hand on his shoulder the Skipper said gravely: "Always remember, James, when you are hunting dangerous game, to look behind you. Never forget that. *Look behind*."

This was a lesson which may have been of service to James when, not many years later, he was hunting enemy aircraft in the war-stricken sky of France. The picture of those terrible jaws open to seize him was too vivid ever to be forgotten.

All his father said about the affair was: "Don't let this go to your head, my boy. You still have a lot to learn before you can call yourself a *shikari*."

In conclusion it should be said that the boy who had been bitten not only recovered but became something of an embarrassment to James, following him about whenever he saw him, smiling and making signs that he was a sort of god. Perhaps it was understandable.

THE BIG BAD BEAR

SHOULD the bear be included in the list of dangerous wild animals? This has long been a subject for discussion between big game hunters. There are arguments for and against. Opinion appears to depend on the experience of each individual. Some, who have never had any trouble with a bear, assert the beast is harmless if left alone. Others, who may have been victims of an unprovoked attack, will not accept this.

The truth may be that it all depends on the particular bear. Generally speaking the bear is an inoffensive family man; but, like many wild animals, when he grows old he is forced to lead a solitary life, and in these conditions he tends to become bad-tempered, morose, ready to go for anyone or anything that disturbs him. There is reason to think he may even go looking for trouble. He will rush out of a thicket and claw a passing native for no apparent reason. Of course, for all we know there may be a reason for this display of foul temper. He may have been stung by a bee; or trodden on a thorn; or may have a belly-ache from eating under-ripe fruit. Whatever the reason, it happens, and an angry bear is not the cuddly creature we see at a zoo.

If Bruin himself is hurt he is liable to set up a howling and bleating that would be comical were it not pathetic.

There are of course many different kinds of bears in various parts of the world, but with a few exceptions their habits, how they live and what they eat, are much the same. Their usual diet consists of roots, fruits, nuts and delicacies when they can be found, such as wild honey. Some will eat fish, or small animals and reptiles. Most of them can climb trees.

Exceptions are the grizzly bear of North America. He will eat carrion. He has been known to charge on sight; hence his ugly reputation. The polar bear is also a flesh eater, but as where he lives there is nothing else he can be forgiven. Both these bears are hard to kill. There are still bears in the forests of Eastern Europe, where, dangerous or not, they are treated with respect.

But here we are only concerned with the two species that occur in India, or to be more specific, in the Himalayas, for it was in an encounter with one of these that young James Bigglesworth came near to losing his life. These two species are known as the "red" and the "black". The red is less dangerous than the black. Both can be carnivorous, sometimes killing sheep or goats, for which reason they are feared and hated by the hill people, some of whom can show terrible scars. Men have been scalped, or had half their face torn off, by one swipe of those terrible claws.

The black bear can easily be recognized by having

a broad white arrow on his chest. His eyesight is not very good, but he has an acute sense of smell, and hearing. His habit is to lie up by day in a thicket or clump of scrub where he would be difficult to see until he rises up and rushes out, either from rage or panic. In a charge he can move at great speed. His usual attack is on all fours, sometimes rising on his hind legs for a better view, finally standing erect to strike blows with his claws rather than use his teeth. One swipe, a sort of vicious hook, can cause a frightful wound. If he can get his "arms" round his adversary he will hug him to death.

He is a big beast, his thick, shaggy coat making him look larger than he is; for which reason he is easy to miss with a rifle shot, the bullet passing through the hair without touching the animal inside it.

Living where he did Biggles heard many stories and rumours about any unusual behaviour of wild animals, this, naturally, always being the topic for gossip; but he thought little about bears, never having encountered one. That he did so eventually came about like this.

He was sitting in the garden, reading, when in walked Captain Lovell, a celebrated big game hunter, whom he now knew well enough to call "Skipper". Wearing a well-worn hunting outfit he was accompanied by an Indian orderly, a gun bearer, carrying his rifle.

James sprang up waving a greeting. "Hello, Skipper, what fair wind brings you here?"

"As I was passing this way I thought I'd better make a courtesy call on your father," was the answer. "Is he at home?"

"Yes. He's in the office. I'll take you through." James led the way to the room where his father was busy on official papers.

"I shan't keep you," the Skipper said. "I'm on my way to Charipur. Thought I'd just look in to pass the time of day."

"Charipur! That's in the hills. It's a fair step."

"There's a rest-house half-way. I shall spend a night there."

"What's the trouble?"

"Nothing serious. I had word from Saunders of the Forestry Service that a bear was making a nuisance of itself and he'd be obliged if I could find time to put an end to it."

"A lot of fuss about nothing, probably."

"Maybe. But apparently this old devil has taken to knocking off sheep, and several people who have tried to stop him have been hurt. The headman had a go, but all he did was wound the beast, since when the footpath between Charipur and Namsala, where the bear hangs out, has been closed. The kids of Charipur have to use the path to get to school. Or they did. Now they can't. It's too dangerous."

"What are you going to do?"

Captain Lovell shrugged a shoulder. "There's only one thing to do with a bear that develops nasty habits and that's kill it. There shouldn't be any difficulty about that, but I'd rather someone else did the job. I don't care much for bear shooting. It's too easy. It may be fun for young officers just out from Home, anxious to get a trophy of some sort to prove they're up to standard, but I've long passed that stage."

"Do you mind if I come with you, sir?" put in James.

His father answered. "Certainly not. You'd only be in the way."

"Oh, let him come if he wants to," protested the Skipper. "He couldn't take any harm. He might bump into a bear himself one day. If he's coming into the Service when he's of age he should know how to handle such a situation. I can show him."

"Oh, very well, if you don't mind."

"Can I take my rifle?" James asked eagerly.

"No."

"I think it would be as well if he had a weapon in his hands—just in case," the Skipper said. "There shouldn't be any trouble, but on these trips one never knows what may crop up. But it's no use fiddling about with a light rifle. If there was trouble it could only make matters worse. It needs something with a real punch to stop a bear."

"You are not, I hope, contemplating allowing this boy to shoot the bear," said James' father, sternly.

"Of course not. I'll do the shooting. But I think it would be advisable to let him have something

c

capable of dealing with an emergency. It would give him confidence."

"All right, if you say so," was the reluctant reply. "He can take my Rigby. That should stop anything."

Having obtained his father's permission for the outing James left the room for fear he might change his mind. Hurrying to his bedroom he changed into more suitable clothes, and with his father's heavy rifle under his arm he went out to the garden where he found Captain Lovell waiting for him.

"Ready?" inquired the Skipper.

"Yes."

"Cartridges?"

"In my pocket." James handed the rifle to the orderly to carry, knowing there was a long and tiring walk ahead. That was why the Indian was there, to carry anything likely to be needed, rations for two or three days, for instance.

The party set off. There was little talking, breath being reserved for the uphill climb, until late in the afternoon when the rest-house was reached. After a rest, a light meal, and preparations for the night complete, the Skipper said: "Sit down, James. I want to talk to you. Whatever I may have said to your father I don't want you to get the impression that hunting a bad-tempered old bear, as apparently this one is, is all fun and games. An angry bear can be an awkward customer. He hasn't a lot of intelligence but he can have a fair share of cunning. Let me give you a tip or two. Remember, if he comes for you, you can't escape by climbing a tree, even if there happens to be one handy. He can climb faster than you. He's had more practice. If you see a bear in a tree leave him alone. He has a trick of sliding down the far side of the trunk, so you can't see him. While you're wondering where he's gone he's suddenly on the ground in front of you, probably prepared to charge. If he comes on all fours aim just below the chin to reach his heart. If he rises up shoot at the bottom point of the white chevron on his chest. Never tackle a bear if he's above you, say, on the slope of a hill. He's not very fast uphill, but coming down he can arrive like a ton of bricks, as the saying is."

"I'll remember what you say," James said seriously.

"I'm not expecting anything like this to happen, but it's as well to be prepared. If the bear has one peculiarity it is this: he's utterly unpredictable. He's liable to do anything. Wounded, he may sit down and howl. He may go on the rampage like a mad bull, or behave as if he doesn't know what the dickens he is doing. The golden rule is, be ready for anything."

"I will," promised James.

With this advice the conversation ended. With night drawing its curtain over the jungle they went to bed.

It was mid-morning the next day when they arrived at the little hill village of Charipur. They were received with open arms, as the saying is, it being supposed, apparently, that the end of the big bad bear was close. James, observing the frightful scars carried by some of the men, was by no means sure of it. The headman himself had a mutilated face, barely healed. James inquired how long this menace had been going on, and was shocked to learn that it was nearly three years. When he asked why no complaint had been made earlier he was informed that the village didn't like to make a fuss over something the people should be able to deal with. So far, obviously, they had failed. Which was not surprising, for their only weapon was an antique, muzzle-loading rifle, likely to be a greater danger to the man who fired it than to the target. The headman, with a ghastly grin, claimed he had wounded the bear with it. James could only admire the courage of a man who would take on a ferocious animal with such a weapon.

The Skipper asked where the bear was usually to be found, adding that he hoped to settle the business that day.

The headman said he would show them. It haunted the path that went round the hill to Namsala.

The orderly, having no weapon, was ordered to wait for them, and watched by the entire village the party of three, Skipper, James and the headman, set off. They had not far to go. They came to a narrow but well-used track, which the headman said was the path to Namsala. It wound round the flank of the hill. The village was on the far side.

Loading his rifle the Skipper told the headman he need come no further. To James he said: "I shall go in front. You follow, keeping close behind me. You can load your rifle but leave the safety catch on. This is the sort of ground, with loose rocks to trip over, where an accident can easily happen. Watch me and don't talk. If I stop, you stop. Don't try to see why I've stopped. Understand?"

"Yes, sir."

"Good. Let's go on."

The slope both above and below the track was almost devoid of vegetation. There were a few patches of dwarf scrub, outcrops of rock and a lot of loose boulders; but there was really nowhere to provide cover for an animal the size of a bear. There were no trees. In fact, the hillside might have been described as "open". But presently this changed. The winding path became so narrow that it was only possible to move in single file. Indeed, the path itself became a hazard.

On the left-hand side the ground, mostly barren rock strewn with boulders, rose sharply to the summit of the hill. On the other side it fell away even more steeply for some distance before ending, as far as could be judged, in a *nullah*, or ravine, its course marked by some tall timber. This slope, too, as steep as the roof of a house, was covered with shale and loose rock, some of it looking as if it only needed a touch to send it crashing down. Here and there the petrified roots of ancient trees projected from the detritus. On the path itself it was seldom possible to see more than thirty or forty yards ahead because of projecting shoulders of rock. The Skipper reconnoitred each one cautiously before rounding it.

The sun was hot. The rock reflected its heat. There was no shade. Stopping once to wipe the sweat from his face the Skipper said: "I don't care much for this. It's hard to imagine a worse place to run into trouble. Keep your eyes skinned. We may have to move fast. If we do, mind you don't slip."

James nodded.

The Skipper went on, rifle at the ready, to the next projecting face of rock that obscured the view beyond it. Reaching it he stopped, peeped round and raised a hand in a beckoning signal to show that the way was clear.

It was at this moment that a slight sound, like the rattle of a rolling pebble, caused James to turn his head to look behind him, thinking they might have started a landslide.

What he saw froze the blood in his veins—if such a thing is possible. It was the bear. Moving fast it was on the path within a few paces of him. Standing on its hind legs it looked enormous, larger than any bear he could have imagined. It seemed to tower above him. Making uncouth noises it was coming on at a shambling run waving its fore-paws.

After the first stunning shock, which for an instant seemed to take the strength out of his limbs, James kept his head. Even as he let out a cry of warning he remembered his safety catch was on. With a swift movement of his thumb he slipped it off, and taking aim at the point of the white chevron on the bear's chest, fired. The range was point blank. The bear should have fallen. But it didn't. With a hoarse bellow, still on its feet it staggered on towards him. It seemed impossible that he could have missed.

Before he could reload the bear was on him, a clawed foot swinging round in a wild swipe at his face. There was no dodging the blow. There was hardly room to move. All James could do was ward off the blow with the rifle, holding it up in both hands. It took the shock, but the force of it caused him to reel backwards. Before he could recover his balance a foot went over the edge of the path. He went over backwards, and the next instant was rolling down the slope clutching frantically for something, anything, that would stop his uncontrolled progress down the hill.

It would be futile to attempt to describe his sensations during the next few seconds, during which time he travelled some forty or fifty yards, before, with a severe jolt, he was brought to a halt by what turned out to be an ancient tree stump.

He had lost hold of his rifle as soon as he felt himself falling—or the bear may have knocked it out of his hands—he didn't know which. Above the noise of crashing rocks from the landslide he had started he was vaguely conscious of shots and a strong smell of bear. Pulling himself into a sitting position he saw the reason. The bear had fallen with him. It had stopped a little below him. It was still alive, and with hate flaming in its eyes, coughing blood-flecked foam, it was scrambling up the slope to get at him.

James tried to drag himself higher by pulling on the stump, but it started to tear loose under the strain and for a moment it looked as if he was going to slide down into the arms of the bear. It was still struggling to get at him, but had obviously been hard hit and was only making slow progress. Prompted by desperation, and maybe the instinct of self-preservation, James reached out for a lump of loose rock rather larger than a coconut. Raising it above his head with both hands he hurled it with all the force he could muster at the bear's head. It struck the animal squarely on the muzzle. Clutching at its face, making a great noise of growling and howling the creature fell on its side. This started another landslide, and bear and rocks went rolling down the hill in a cloud of dust finally to disappear from sight over the lip of the *nullah*.

For a minute James sat still, panting and sweating from excitement and exertion, trying to muster enough strength to take stock of his position. A shout made him look up. The Skipper stood poised on the brink of the slope. He called: "Are you all right?"

James managed to answer yes.

"Then try to get up here," said the Skipper. "If I try to get down to you I may set more rocks rolling and one might hit you on the head."

James raised a hand to show that he understood and then started laboriously to make his way back up to the path. Just before reaching the top, to his great relief he came on his rifle. The Skipper helped him on to the path, where for a little while he sat still to recover his breath and his faculties. When at last he was able to speak he said: "Did you say something about bear hunting being a sport for amateurs?"

"I also said bears were unpredictable. You've just seen a good example. What happened?"

"He came along the path behind us. If he hadn't made a noise he'd have caught me before I knew he was there. When I looked round he was practically breathing down my neck. I only had time for one quick shot. I aimed where you told me; but he didn't drop. He made a swipe and knocked me off the path."

The Skipper nodded. "I saw that. I couldn't shoot for fear of hitting you. When you fell he came on at me. I gave him a couple of shots; his rush carried him over the edge of the path and he followed you down the hill. At one time you were rolling together. There was nothing I could do."

"I didn't really know what was happening. It was all so sudden."

"I can well understand that. The cunning old

devil must have seen us go past. He didn't move. He waited till he could get between us and the village to stop us going back. Well, he won't try that trick again. He must be dead by now. If your shot didn't kill him mine will. I'm sorry this had to happen. I was careless."

"I don't see how you could be expected to know what the old brute was going to do," James said. "You'd better not tell my father about this or he may not let me go out with you again. Thank goodness I found his rifle. I wouldn't have dared to go home without it."

The Skipper was looking back along the track. "I can see the headman. He must have heard the shooting and has come along to see what has happened." He shouted to the man, who was peeping round a rock: "The bear's dead. You'll find him in the *nullah*."

The man disappeared with alacrity.

"If you feel up to it we'll get back to the village where my orderly can make us a cup of tea," the Skipper said. "We can't reach home today but we should be able to get as far as the rest-house. The village men will bring in the bear, no doubt. Do you want the skin for a trophy?"

"No thanks," James answered emphatically. "I'm nothing for collecting heads or hides. I shall remember today without a reminder. I've enough bumps and bruises to help my memory for a while, anyway."

They made their way slowly back to the village

where they were soon refreshing themselves with hot tea. A great noise of triumphant shouting heralded the return of the men who had gone to the *nullah* to bring in the body of the bear that had harassed them for so long.

Looking at it James remarked: "It doesn't look so big now it's dead."

The Skipper made a wry face. "They never do. It's not the size that matters, it's what they do. Anyhow, the kids can now go back to school and get on with their lessons."

"I've had one myself, today, if it comes to that," James said thoughtfully. "Did I do anything wrong?"

The Skipper smiled. "I couldn't have done better myself. You kept your head, that's the important thing. It would have been easy to lose it. You'll pass."

And that was the end of James' first encounter with a bear.

THE ONE THAT GOT AWAY

Young James Bigglesworth knew a lot about snakes. He had to know. Living where he did it could hardly be otherwise. While these dangerous creatures formed part of ordinary everyday existence they were also a subject for common gossip, particularly when someone was bitten. James not only heard talk of snakes but sometimes saw one, venomous or otherwise. In India there are many species of snakes but not all are poisonous.

And then, of course, there were the snake charmers, those strange men who appear to exercise control over the reptiles. They occurred in two sorts. There were those who used them for a form of entertainment. They would appear in the bazaar with a basket of cobras or Russell vipers, both extremely poisonous, and by playing a tune on a reed instrument cause them to sway to the music in a sort of ballet dance. There were sceptics who said the snakes had had their poison glands removed. Biggles didn't know about that. He didn't care. It fascinated him to see the fearless way the deadly creatures were handled.

The other cult of snake charmers were different. They were usually holy men and they took their business seriously. If anyone suspected he had a snake on the premises, perhaps in the thatch, he would send for one of these men. The charmer would come and call out the snake. If there was one within hearing distance it would appear. He would put it in a bag and take it away. These men did not kill snakes. There was a mystery about this which James never understood.

He once saw a boy killed by a *krait*. He was weeding in the garden. He was struck. He did a strange thing. Perhaps realizing he was doomed he seized the snake and in a fury tore it to pieces with his teeth. So they both died.

On another occasion he saw a snake kill a dog. He knew this snake by sight. It was a *hamadryad*, sometimes called the King Cobra. It is yellow with black crossbands and can grow to a length of twelve feet. This one lived in a village he knew and in spite of a reputation for ferocity it appeared to be harmless. There existed a sort of truce between the snake and the villagers. They did not interfere with it and it did not molest them. Some villagers actually welcome the presence of this questionable visitor asserting that it will keep down the rats; a sort of house cat. It may be true.

At all events, one day James was passing through the village and paused to look at this particular beast as it lay in the open, coiled up, basking in the sun. At this moment a dog appeared, evidently a stranger to the place. Spotting the snake, making a lot of noise it flew at it.

Snakes are commonly regarded as sluggish, slow-moving creatures, but the speed at which this one moved was an eye-opener to James. It made for its lair, a hole under a tree, at such a rate that the dog had difficulty in overtaking it. It succeeded just as the snake dived into its hole. The dog managed to get hold of the end of its tail and tried to drag it out. In a flash the snake's head reappeared It struck. Its fangs sank into the dog's neck. The dog retired, silent. In two or three minutes it was staggering about as if it was drunk. Five more minutes and it had died in convulsions.

James went on his way pondering what he had seen and more than ever determined to keep out of long grass, where snakes are often found.

He had one experience with a snake that he was never likely to forget.

It was a hot day. He was at home, lazing in a deck-chair in the shade of some trees near the road. He was bored. His father was away and he had nothing to do. He had been told to rest following a mild attack of his recurrent fever. This had left him feeling rather weak, the palms of his hands still damp from the temperature he had been running. The house was silent. The dusty road was deserted. The overheated air quivered.

He was gazing at the road in a disinterested sort of way when a boy appeared. He was running, which in such weather could only mean his errand was urgent. James recognized him as Sula Dowla, a lad of about his own age, son of the assistant native overseer at a nearby tea estate a little way up on the hillside. They had sometimes been out together. To James' surprise Sula dashed straight into the garden. He was breathless and obviously excited. "Come," he said in a tense voice.

"What's the hurry?" inquired James without moving, not feeling inclined for anything that demanded exertion.

"Come. Come quick," was the answer.

"Come where, and why?" asked James, without enthusiasm.

"Now we make some money," declared Sula.

"How?"

"Bring rifle. I show you."

"How do we make money with a rifle?"

"Come. We waste time."

Reluctantly James went into the house, took his rifle from the rack, put a handful of cartridges in his pocket and rejoined his dark-skinned companion.

"Now, what's all this about?" he wanted to know.

"You will see." Sula set off the way he had come.

James shrugged and followed. It did not occur to him that there was any danger or Sula would not have been so anxious to return. Two or three times as they walked up the hill to the tea plantation James asked to be told what they were going to do; but all he got from Sula, with a mysterious smile, was: "You'll see."

Later on James thought he should have guessed the truth. The proposal to make some money

should have provided a clue. At this period the
latest fashion in ladies' shoes, in the capitals of
Europe, was snakeskin, and as there was a limit to
the amount of material available they were expensive. Skins were in demand and a good one
could fetch up to ten pounds. However, James
was not thinking of shoes, and fashion was the last
thing in his mind.

When they arrived at the tea estate he saw at
once that something was amiss. Women who
should have been working were huddled in a
group, obviously apprehensive, looking in their
direction.

Sula led the way to one of the several drainage
or irrigation ditches that crossed the plantation.
These were narrow slit trenches about eighteen
inches wide and from two to three feet deep.
Again, later James thought he had been slow not
to realize what was afoot, for to the best of his
knowledge there was only one creature likely to
seek shelter from the sun in such a place. Indeed,
he had been warned that these trenches, dark,
damp and cool, were often used by snakes to lie in
during the heat of the day. So he really had little
excuse for what was to follow; but for some reason
he forgot.

Sula approached the trench on tip-toe. He
beckoned. He pointed down. He made a sign that
might have meant anything and backed away.
James advanced. He peered. He looked. He
stared. At first he could see nothing except the

criss-crossed pattern of shadows cast by the over-hanging grasses that flourished along the edge of the trench. They broke up the background at the bottom.

Then, suddenly, he saw it. What he actually saw was two unwinking eyes that glared balefully into his own. He realized instantly that he was looking at the head of a snake. His eyes followed the body, lying flat along the bottom of the trench. He thought it would never end, and his heart missed a beat when he perceived he was looking at an enormous python, the largest snake in India, if not in the world, with a body that can exceed thirty feet in length. Now Sula's curious behaviour was explained. And the women's.

James' instant reaction was to remove himself as quickly as possible from the locality. If this was Sula's idea of getting some easy money it was not his. If the Indian boy wanted the skin he could get it himself, for to enter into an argument with such a formidable creature was not seriously to be con-templated. Not as far as James was concerned, anyway.

Apparently the monster was lying quiet, and James asked no more than it would continue to do so. He resolved not to interfere. He knew of course that the python is not poisonous; that it kills by constriction; that is, by coiling itself round its victim and crushing it to death before swallowing it whole. He had also been told that when it attacks a python moves with the speed of a spring released from tension. So, for more reasons than one James was content to let sleeping dogs lie, or should we say, leave a quiet snake alone.

"Shoot," urged Sula, taking care to stand well clear, but apparently still thinking of the value of the skin.

"No," answered James, firmly. He could have done with some money, but he could think of easier ways than this to get it.

Without looking behind him he stepped backwards. There was a brittle crack as something snapped. A cry broke from his lips as a terrible pain shot up the calf of his leg. He sank down thinking he had been shot; but when he tried to get up he realized what had happened. He had put his heel on an old rotten tree stump. A piece had broken off short so that the entire weight of his body had been thrown on the muscle, or a tendon, in his calf. This had snapped. He had heard it. Only those to whom this has happened know what it means. To put any weight on the leg is out of the question. The agony is excruciating, not to be borne. As James quickly realized when he tried to stand. He began to crawl away from the spot.

A warning shout from Sula made him look round. The python was gliding out of the trench, yard after yard of it, endlessly as it seemed.

Sick with pain James crawled faster. Or he tried. Sula, with his eyes on the snake, rushed forward to help him. He caught his toe on the same stump that had been the cause of James' downfall

and went headlong, knocking James flat. He was
quickly on his feet, his eyes popping out of his head,
to use the common expression. And no wonder.
The python, head raised, tongue flickering, was
coming straight towards them. He hesitated.

"Run," gasped James.

Sula's answer was to snatch up the rifle James
had dropped.

"No! Don't shoot," yelled James, near panic.
He didn't know what Sula's marksmanship was
like and was afraid that if he wounded the mon-
strous reptile he would only make matters worse.
There was also some risk that in his frantic haste
Sula might shoot *him*.

James, unable to move, sat still. Sula, by this
time quite beside himself, screamed at the snake,
although what good he thought this would do only
he knew. Perhaps he didn't know. In the distance
the women, who could see what was happening,
also started screaming. All this noise may have
had some effect. Anyhow, the python glided on,
taking not the slightest notice of the boys apart
from hissing its displeasure. It passed so close to
James that he could have touched it. He noticed
a great swelling in the middle of its beautifully-
marked body. This, as was explained to him
presently, was probably the reason for the snake's
behaviour. It had recently had a meal and had
been lying in the trench to digest it, which may
take some time.

At all events, suddenly it was all over. The

snake, to the unspeakable relief of both boys, went on past them to disappear from sight in the tea shrubs. Pale, weak and shaking, they watched it go.

It was at this juncture that Sula's father, brought to the spot by the screaming, came running up. He was just in time to see the end of the business. It was he who explained the probable cause of the python's lethargic conduct. Why it had left the trench was a matter for surmise. It may have been the sound of human voices close to it. It may have been sleeping when Sula first saw it, its presence having been revealed to him by the women who had seen the creature go into the ditch.

On this occasion James had to be carried home on an improvised stretcher. He walked with crutches for a fortnight and limped for a long time afterwards. The easy money Sula had anticipated did not materialize. James told him in no uncertain terms that he'd have to find an easier way to get some.

What his father had to say about it when he returned home, for of course James had to account for his injury, can perhaps be left to the imagination.

A SORT OF EDUCATION

There is no record of the first occasion when young
James Bigglesworth found it necessary to kill something; but living where he did when he was a boy,
on the fringe of the jungle country in the United
Provinces of India, then under British rule, with
pests, some of them dangerous, finding their way
into the garden and even into the house, it is likely
that his experience in this respect began when he
was quite small.

We know he had at least two early escapes from
sudden death from what was, and still is, the most
common peril in rural India: snake-bite; which
accounts for thousands of deaths every year. This
can happen anywhere at any time, for some of the
most deadly Indian snakes are so small and incon-
spicuous that they can creep unnoticed into the
most unlikely places. The risk of this is such a
common occurrence that one becomes accustomed
to it and soon thinks no more about it. It is accepted
as a hazard as traffic is regarded in a city.

Of course, when a narrow escape does occur the
shock serves as a rude reminder of what can happen.
One has to learn to take care, to think fast or take
the consequences.

James had such a shock when he was a mere nine

years of age. He went to the bathroom. The door had been left ajar. When he pushed it open, a *krait*, a small but one of the deadliest of the Indian snakes, which must have been lying on top, fell off and landed on his shoulder, a position from which, luckily, it bounced off on to the floor. In one jump James was back through the doorway. The snake tried to leave at the same time. As it struck at him he slammed the door on it and broke its back.

He had another lucky escape when, intending to take a walk over some rough ground, he picked up his high "mosquito" boots to pull them on. One felt curiously heavy. Thinking some object had been accidentally dropped in it he was within an ace of inserting a hand to ascertain what it was. Instead, fortunately, he took the simplest way to find out by turning the boot upside down. Out fell a cobra which, for reasons best known to itself, must have decided the boot was a ready-made hole. He killed it with the old golf club, a putter, which he sometimes carried as a walking stick. He found it handy for swatting small creatures with nasty habits.

One day he killed another *krait* with the same instrument. Wearing only shorts and tennis shoes he had been "chipping" a golf ball about the garden. It had rolled into a weedy flower bed. Using the stick to part the weeds in order to find it he became aware of something creeping up his leg. Glancing down he saw with a thrill of horror that it was a *krait*. Its head was held back as if to strike.

James didn't stop to think; to wonder what to do. There was no time for that. Nor did he lose his head. What he did may have been an instinctive reaction to peril. Taking the club by the iron, with the shaft, regardless of his leg, he struck the snake with all his force. The venomous creature fell off and he jumped clear. Then he beat it to death. Only then did he realize how hard he had struck. For a month he carried a livid blue and black bruise down his calf.

He did not regard these events as adventures. They were the hazards of his every-day life.

Curiously, perhaps, one of his narrowest escapes from what might have been a fatal accident involved a dog. It was not an ordinary dog as dogs are generally understood in England. It was a *pariah*. Actually, a *pariah* is the name given to the lowest class of Indian, shunned by everyone. A *pariah*-dog is the same thing in the canine population; an ownerless mongrel, an outcast. They are common in the East. Normally, acting as scavengers they do little harm. The real trouble with the one in question was, it was in the throes of hydrophobia, commonly called rabies, a hideous disease which as the result of strict quarantine laws has almost disappeared in Britain.

An animal suffering from it goes raving mad, foaming at the mouth, and in this condition it will attack anybody or anything with the greatest ferocity, going always for the throat or the face. A person, or certain animals, so bitten will catch the disease with the same result. What makes it almost impossible to eradicate in the East is the fact that wild animals, such as jackals, which may hang about the outskirts of a town, may have the disease. Should they encounter a dog and bite it that dog will almost inevitably develop rabies and pass it on to any human with whom it comes in contact.

The circumstances in which James became involved with a rabid dog were these. He was sitting on the verandah of his father's bungalow when from on the road, not far away, came a series of screams. Running to the gate to ascertain the reason the explanation was instantly apparent. Less than forty yards away a young Indian girl was being attacked by a dog; a heavily-built brute of the lurcher type. Her dress was already in shreds and she was trying to fend it off with the remains of what had been a laundry basket. The insane behaviour of the dog made it evident that it was a victim of rabies. James recognized the girl as the pretty daughter of their *dhobi-wallah* (an Indian laundryman) who did the linen for the house.

He was not so foolish as to take on the rabid dog with his bare hands. He tore back to the house, snatched the nearest rifle—a .22 repeater—from its rack, grabbed some loose cartridges from the table drawer and, loading as he ran, raced back to the road.

He found the position more or less unchanged. The girl, no longer screaming, was fighting desperately to keep the dog off by slashing at it, or trying to smother it, with wet sheets. The ground was strewn with rags. No one had arrived to help her. This was understandable. To tackle the raving animal with anything less efficient than a firearm would have been idiotic, probably suicidal.

James ran towards the scene shouting to attract the dog's attention and so perhaps give the girl a chance to get away. He succeeded better than he intended. The dog abandoned the girl and rushed at him in a frenzy, eyes wild, teeth bared, jaws slavering froth.

James stopped, took quick aim—perhaps too quick—and fired. A spurt of dust beside the dog told him that the shot had missed. He had to be more careful because the animal was more or less in line with the girl. He shouted to her to run but she seemed incapable of movement. With the dog now less than a dozen yards away he jerked another cartridge into the breech and fired again. Still the dog came on, although from the way it stumbled he knew he had hit it but obviously not in a vital place.

He just had time to reload and the dog was at him, snapping. There was no question of taking aim. He fired point blank from the hip. The dog did a somersault, fell and for a moment lay twitching. Then it got to its feet again and James had to do some quick side-stepping to avoid the clashing jaws. He reloaded as he did so. Then, thrusting the muzzle of the rifle almost into the dog's mouth he pulled the trigger.

That did it. The cur rolled over and after some final convulsions lay still. He put another bullet through its brain to make sure. Then, satisfied it was dead, he hurried to the girl who still stood trembling amid the rags of the garments she had been carrying.

"Did it bite you?" he asked tersely.

"No, *sahib*," gasped the girl.

"Are you sure?"

"Yes."

"Not a scratch anywhere?"

"No." She showed her bare arms and legs to prove it. Then, crying, she began to collect her washing.

"Never mind those," James said, noticing she had been splashed with foam from the dog's mouth. "Go home at once and have a bath."

"Yes, *sahib*."

By now several people were hurrying towards them. The first to arrive was the girl's father, incoherent and nearly hysterical.

"Take her home and make sure there isn't a mark on her," ordered James curtly. Then, as the man fell on his knees at James' feet, calling down the blessings of heaven on him, he cut in abruptly. "Never mind about that. Take her home. Then fetch the dog and burn it—and mind you don't scratch yourself on its teeth or claws."

James' father strode up. "I heard shots," he said. He looked at the dead dog; then at James. "Did you do this?" he inquired.

"Yes, sir."

"Hm. How did it happen?"

"I saw the dog attacking the girl so I fetched a rifle and shot it."

"You should have called me, or one of the men."

"There wasn't time. As it was I thought I'd be too late."

"Is that rifle still loaded?"

"Er—yes."

"Then unload at once. It's dangerous to stand about with a loaded firearm. That's how accidents happen."

James obeyed.

"Is the girl all right?" asked his father.

"Yes. Not a scratch on her as far as I could see. I've told her father to collect these rags and burn the body of the dog."

"Quite right. These *pariahs* are a curse. If this should happen again, fetch me. Understand?"

"Yes, sir," answered James, obediently.

If he got nothing else out of this encounter he won the undying gratitude of the *dhobi-wallah* and the devotion of his daughter. It may be, too, that it was this sort of education that taught him to think fast, act, and remain calm in moments of extreme danger.

A month after this affair he was on his way to England, to school. He never saw his father again. Many years were to pass before he had the unforgettable smell of India in his nostrils. When he left her shores he was still a boy with no suspicion of what the future held, of the war that was to change his life, of the still more deadly perils that awaited him in the skies of a stricken Europe. When he returned it was as a battle-scarred veteran.

LIVING DANGEROUSLY

Young James Bigglesworth had several nasty experiences when he was certainly not looking for trouble. They may not have been as desperate as some but they provided moments of acute anxiety.

It seems that no matter where one lives there is no escaping the risk of death or mutilation by accident. In the wilder parts of what are called the undeveloped countries the hazards of life are natural and must always have been so. In cities where the chance of being struck by a snake, or mauled by a wild animal, is non-existent, the danger is provided by man-made devices like mechanical transportation.

It must not be imagined that James encountered a dangerous beast every time he went out. Of course not. Weeks could go past without an incident worth mentioning. But it could happen, and on occasion did happen, perhaps when least expected; wherefore it became a way of life always to be on the alert.

Something could go wrong on what appeared to be a simple ramble, and an example of this is provided by James' first adventure with a buffalo. Many countries have this animal although it may have different names according to locality. Bison in America, for instance. But they are all members of the same family; not very handsome creatures, perhaps, but with a common reputation for courage, ferocity when wounded, and for being hard to kill.

In Biggles' part of India there were not many buffalo. Their numbers had been decreasing for some time, and before a hunter could shoot one he had to obtain a licence. They were largely forest animals, shy, with a wonderful faculty for standing dead still, which made them very hard to see; but they had a habit of moving out to open ground to find grazing and water. For the most part they did little harm. Sometimes a native would be injured by one, which was probably his own fault. They kept together in small herds and would usually fade away silently at the approach of a man.

The exception might be an old bull which, becoming morose, had gone solitary and kept to his ground. Herds posted sentries, a duty undertaken by old cows. James had once or twice seen some in the distance, or heard them, or noticed their "marks"; but having no great interest in them he never interfered. His encounter with one was not of his seeking. It was an old bull. If he was an evil-tempered old man he had reason for it. But James was not to know that. This is how it happened.

He was out for a walk one day with his young Indian friend, Habu Din. He carried his light rifle, not because he expected to use it as they were unlikely to see dangerous game. He took it "just in case", and for that reason he put only two or three cartridges in his pocket. It might be useful to kill a cobra. He already knew from conversations with hunters that to take on a large and dangerous beast with a light-calibre weapon was folly. A big animal needs a heavy bullet to bring it down; that is, to kill it outright. Such creatures have tremendous vitality.

Habu Din had told James about a place he had found, where the river ran through more or less open ground, where the flowers were marvellous. He painted a picture of a sort of earthly paradise. James was not particularly interested in flowers, but the place seemed to offer an object, as good as any, for an excursion. So they went.

Before arriving at the objective James was regretting that he had allowed himself to be induced to undertake the trip. Habu had taken him through a strip of virgin jungle; and that was bad enough. On emerging they were faced with an open tract of land with isolated trees dotted about here and there. Habu said they were only going across to the far side. But to get there meant forcing a way through long grass and rushes, sometimes waist high. There was no suggestion of a track, and at every step they disturbed swarms of flies and other insects to settle on James' perspiring face. More than once he was tempted to call a halt and abandon the whole expedition. It wasn't worth the effort. But rather than disappoint Habu he struggled on, although in the event they never did reach their objective.

They were about half way across when some small dark birds rose into the air, twittering, a little way in front of them. James came to a stop. He knew what they were. Tick-birds. That is, birds that feed on the bugs, grubs and insects that bury themselves in the hides of animals. Many large wild creatures have them, and are glad to accommodate them because they serve two useful purposes. They clear their skins of parasites and at the same time act as sentinels, rising into the air with warning cries on the approach of danger.

So James knew the presence of the birds could only mean one thing, although so far he was unable to see anything. He laid a restraining hand on the bare brown arm of his companion. "Wait," he whispered. "There must be something there." Not that Habu really needed telling. He must have known the signs as well as James.

They advanced slowly for a pace or two, peering cautiously ahead. It was enough. James could see as much as he needed to know. Level with the top of the grass was a massive head decorated with a pair of enormous spreading horns. An old bull buffalo, apparently lying down. It had seen them. With its nose raised and horns laid well back, as is its habit, it was gazing straight at them. It must have heard them coming, even if it hadn't caught their taint, for the buffalo has an abnormally acute sense of smell.

James had not a moment's hesitation about what they should do. He wanted nothing to do with the animal. If the beast was lying quietly, as it appeared, he was content not to disturb it. So he began to back away, hoping the matter would end there. After all, they had done nothing to upset the creature. Habu also retired, rather more hurriedly. Then he must have lost his head, for he broke into a run, which was understandable but stupid, because almost any animal will pursue something which it thinks is running away from it. Thus will a dog often chase after a bicycle, or motor bike.

After a few steps James looked back. The buffalo was on its feet. A few more steps and he looked again. The buffalo was walking after them. It was not charging, or anything like that. Just walking, nose thrust forward, advancing at a steady but purposeful walk. A few more yards and again James looked back. The buffalo was now trotting.

This was too much for Habu. He broke into a sprint, as far as that was possible. Knowing it was impossible to reach the cover of the jungle James shouted: "Make for a tree." Whether or not Habu heard him he did not know, for he, too, was now making flat out for the nearest tree. He had no intention of trying to stop an irate buffalo with a light rifle. Another quick glance revealed that the animal had decided to follow him, rather than Habu. Perhaps it was because in a white linen suit he was more conspicuous. Habu, brown-skinned, wore only a loin-cloth.

D

James just managed to reach his selected tree
with the buffalo now at full gallop after him.
Hanging the rifle over his shoulder by the sling,
for he was afraid that if he left it on the ground the
heavy beast would tread on it and damage it, he
went up to the first convenient fork. From there he
looked down. The buffalo glared up at him with
bloodshot eyes. It banged on the tree with its horns
but must have decided it was too robust to be
knocked down. It walked twice round the tree;
then, presumably because tree climbing was not its
line, it lay down. Now James saw the probable
reason for the old bull's behaviour. Its neck and
flanks were streaked with blood. Claw marks.
Only a tiger, or possibly a leopard, could have done
that. No wonder the wretched beast was out to be
revenged on something; on anything.

Of course, James now hoped the buffalo would
go away. But no. It settled down as if prepared to
wait indefinitely. What to do James did not know.
Indeed, there appeared to be nothing he could do.
Looking around for Habu he could see him in
another tree, at a safe distance, watching the
proceedings.

James now gave the problem some earnest
thought. For more reasons than one he didn't
want to be stuck in the tree all day; possibly all
night. For a long while he did nothing, still hoping
the animal would go away; and all the time his
perch was becoming more and more untenable.
The heat of the sun, now approaching its zenith,

fell on him as if blown from the open door of a
furnace. And that was not his only trouble. To
add to his discomfort all the flies in India, perhaps
attracted by the smell of blood, appeared to have
arrived on the spot. They formed a buzzing
curtain around not only the buffalo but the human
being in the tree. James tried to fight them off, but
it was no use. They clung to his face, filled his ears,
eyes and nostrils. Fixed as he was there was no
escaping their persistent attentions. They drove
him nearly frantic.

At long last, when the buffalo showed no sign of
moving he decided something would have to be
done unless he was to lose his sanity. There was,
he thought, one possible remedy for the situation
although he had been loath to consider it. His
rifle. He didn't want to kill the poor beast although
injured as it was he feared it would eventually die.
Actually, he doubted if he would be able to kill it,
but it struck him that a shot might induce it to
leave him. He had no soft-nosed bullets so he
resolved to see what a solid steel-tipped bullet
would do. With the animal so close and looking
up at him he had an easy target.

Brushing flies from his sweating face he took
careful aim at the hard skull between the great
curving horns. He was out of luck. At the precise
moment that he squeezed the trigger the buffalo
chose to move its head, with the result that the
bullet struck the tip of a horn, doing no more
damage than knock a chip off it. The buffalo

merely shook its head. James put in another cartridge and tried again. He heard the smack of the bullet, but as he half expected it simply ricocheted off with a shrill whine. It appeared to have no effect at all. This got him really worried because he found he had only one cartridge left. One chance. Angrily he told himself that never again would he go out with insufficient ammunition. He had learned another lesson.

He put his last cartridge in the breech. This time there should be no mistake. If he killed the animal it would be just too bad, but by now he was getting desperate and in no mood to be too particular. This time he took for his mark a spot just behind the shoulder which should reach the heart. He fired. *Click*. The cartridge had misfired. Such a thing had never happened to him before. Thus he learned that such things can, and do, happen. He turned the cartridge in the breech so that the striker would fall on a different place. He fired again. Another *click*. Six times he tried the cartridge before giving up in disgust. He could only conclude it was a "dud".

Now almost in despair, sick with annoyance and frustration, he sat back on his uncomfortable perch. He looked across at Habu, still in his tree, and yelled to him to go for help. But Habu did not move. Either he did not understand or he was taking no chances with the buffalo, for which he could not be blamed, for he would have to cover the best part of two hundred yards to reach the

nearest point of safety. He was at least safe where
he was.

How this state of affairs would have ended is a
matter for speculation had not help arrived from
an unexpected quarter, although James did not
see it as such when it first appeared. For some time
two vultures had been circling overhead, gradually
coming lower. They now settled in the top of the
tree above James' head. Did they think the buffalo
was dead? Had they, by that uncanny instinct
they possess, been brought to the spot by the sight
or smell of blood? James neither knew nor cared.
All he knew was, if these disgusting scavengers
were looking for a meal they were likely to be
disappointed.

After a while they flapped down and settled on
the ground near the buffalo. Then they began to
hop cautiously towards it. James watched without
any particular interest until the animal began to
show signs of irritation, throwing its head about
as if to indicate that it was not ready to be eaten.
No doubt it knew perfectly well what the birds were
after. This went on for some time, the birds gradually drawing closer with the instinct they have for
imminent death, the stricken beast making furious
sweeps at them with his horns. When two more
arrived to join the original pair apparently the
buffalo could stand it no longer. It rose to its feet
and shook itself. It made one short rush at its
tormentors, and then, without so much as a glance
at the boy in the tree, walked slowly away. The

ugly birds, realizing their anticipated meal was not ready, flapped off, still keeping watch on the buffalo.

James waited until the beast was at a safe distance and then, dropping from his perch, ran for his life as fast as the rank vegetation would permit. Habu, who must have seen what had happened, joined him, and they ran on together without wasting breath in unnecessary conversation. There was no suggestion of resuming the trip to Habu's beauty spot that had been the original objective. James was only too happy to have the chance to turn his back on it. He told Habu so, in no uncertain terms.

As it happened no harm was done, but the incident demonstrates how easily an accident could happen.

Another example, that might have had consequences just as serious, concerned a pig; that is, a wild boar, which in India is commonly called "pig"; hunting this animal on horseback with a spear—a dangerous sport—being known as pig-sticking. The ferocity of this animal when provoked must be seen to be believed. It will fight to its last dying breath. It has been known to try to climb up a spear that has impaled it to get at the man holding the weapon. With razor-like tusks as well as teeth it is a formidable adversary. James, of course, knew all about this reputation, so it will readily be understood that he took care to keep well clear of any place where one might lurk.

They were not common but there was always a chance of one being on open ground near patches of cultivation.

One morning James was out for a stroll to get a breath of cool fresh air before the heat of the day. He chose a well-trodden path that he had always regarded as perfectly safe, for which reason he carried no weapon of any sort, being confident that one would not be needed. Perhaps this was as well; had he carried a rifle he might have been tempted to use it, in which case anything could have happened.

The path led to a small field of millet tended by a man, an Indian of course, who lived in a cottage close to the path and not far from his work. As James passed the primitive cottage this man's wife was at the door grinding some corn. He passed the time of day with her and wandered on, finding the walk very pleasant with no one about to cause a disturbance.

He had not gone far when he saw a movement ahead on the path. When he came to it, it turned out to be a piglet that could not have been more than two or three days old. At such an age it could hardly be dangerous. He stopped. He smiled. He spoke to it. Then, unthinkingly, for he meant no harm to the little creature, he picked it up to look at it more closely. This was too much for the piglet. It squealed with fright, as might have been expected.

Instantly, from some bushes not far away, came

a crash and an answering snort. James did not wait to see what it was. He knew, or guessed, it was the piglet's mother.

He dropped the baby and ran for his life, his objective being the only refuge in sight; the cottage he had just passed. He thought that if he gave the sow her child back she would be content. But no. He could hear her thundering along behind him fairly shrieking with fury.

It is unlikely that James ever covered a hundred yards in faster time. It was a close thing. He reached the cottage with the sow on his heels. The woman was not there, but fortunately the door was wide open. He dashed in and slammed it in the raging animal's face. Then, as there was no chair, he collapsed on the floor to recover his breath, with the woman staring at him in wide-eyed amazement.

The sow snorted about outside for a little while and then went off, presumably to return to her infant, leaving James to explain and make his apologies to the startled woman for his unceremonious entry into her house.

She could understand his haste.

THE THUGS

THE word "thug" has come into the English language to mean a particularly nasty villain, a thief, a rogue, a man who commits robbery with violence, even murder. A man without scruple. The word came to us from India.

The original Thugs were wandering bands of fanatics who infested Central and Northern India and made a definite business of murder. This went on to the present century, when determined efforts had to be made to wipe them out. The operation was partly, but not entirely successful. When caught these inhuman monsters had to be imprisoned for life, otherwise, as was learned from experience, as soon as they were released they resumed their evil calling. It was called Thuggery.

It had in part a religious purpose. The murdered persons and their belongings were held by the Thugs to be a sacrifice to a pagan goddess named Kali. In Biggles' day the larger bands of these tribesmen had been broken up, but they still moved about in ones and twos and these carried on a career of singularly brutal murder.

Their usual method of killing was by slow strangulation. They did not attack a proposed victim openly as one would expect of ordinary

savages. Therein lay their danger. They posed as
quiet, inoffensive people, and in this manner
worked their way into the confidence of the unsuspecting person selected for death. They were
patient and might spend weeks doing this. Then,
one night, usually when he was asleep, they would
fall on the victim, choke him to death and make off
with all he possessed. More barbarous people never
existed.

As we have said, by Biggles' day they had almost
been exterminated, so much so that although stories
of their atrocities sometimes reached his ears he
never gave them a second thought. He knew there
were still a few about, mostly working as indi-
viduals, but he certainly never expected to come into
contact with one, and never even regarded them as
a danger as far as he was concerned. He was on
the friendliest terms with the Indians he knew, no
matter what their caste might be. It was probably
for this reason that when he did encounter one
he was caught off guard. But for something
in the nature of a fluke he might well have lost his
life.

Not all his adventures were with wild animals or
reptiles and this was a case in point. Actually, on
this occasion he was rather naughty, taking an un-
warranted risk. But the reader must judge for himself. Had his father not been away at the time it
would not have happened; but his father had gone
to Lucknow on official business so there was no one
in the house to restrain his impetuosity.

It was a pleasant day, not too hot. James, having completed some self-imposed lessons in the house, decided to take a stroll. For no particular reason he chose the well-used track that ran up the hill to the tea plantations and the forest area beyond. His plan was to go as far as the tea estates where he might chance upon and exchange news with a boy he knew, named Sula Dowla, whose father was an assistant overseer. This track was perfectly safe, for which reason he carried only a walking stick, a light bamboo cane. He had no intention of going beyond the tea gardens. There he would rest a while and return home in time for lunch. That was the plan, and up to a point it worked well enough.

He walked slowly up the hill, steep in places, and in due course reached his objective. He looked around. He could see women working, but they were some distance away so he did not speak to them. He could not see Sula. He waited under a tree for some time and when he did not appear he began the return journey. It was now, really, on the steep part of the hill, that the trouble began.

He came on an old man (or to James he looked old) sitting beside the road with a rather heavy pack beside him. Apparently he had found this a burden and had sat down to rest. James noticed an ugly scar on his chin. He would have passed on without stopping had the man not spoken. From his rather dark skin he took him to be a Gond. (One of the original tribes of India. They have dark skins and

black, curly hair.) The man smiled amiably, and
putting his hands together raised them to his forehead in the customary formal salute. He said something, but James did not catch what it was. That
was why he stopped; to ask the man to repeat what
he had said. He spoke, naturally, in Hindi. The man
answered in the same language, but haltingly, and
with a strange accent, as if the tongue was unfamiliar.
James next tried him in Urdu, another common
language, of which he had some knowledge, but this
was worse. However, somehow they managed to
make themselves understood.

As a matter of courtesy more than for any other
reason James asked the old man where he was going
and what he was doing, for, as far as he knew, apart
from the tea estate the track led to nowhere in
particular, but eventually disappeared in the forest
or in the higher ground beyond. The man's answer
was that he was on his way home, in the mountains,
which James thought explained his unusual way of
speaking. At the moment, the man said, he was
waiting for a friend who had promised to join him to
help him with his pack. He moved aside a little on
the bank to make room and invited the *sahib* to sit
beside him to keep him company and he would tell
him the story of his travels.

Rather than hurt the old man's feelings James
accepted. He was always willing to learn more
about the country from an aspect other than his
own. So they talked for some time, the man
doing most of the talking and James listening. At

length, seeing that time was getting on, and thinking he had done as much as common courtesy demanded, James said he would have to move on. Whereupon the man also said he would have to be on his way. He would wait for his friend no longer, although how he would manage alone, with a pack, he did not know. James saw in this an implied request for help; but not being prepared to go as far as that he made excuses, saying he would have to hurry home as he was already late. It did cross his mind to wonder if the old man was trying to detain him, and if so, why.

At this moment Sula Dowla arrived on the scene, saying he had heard James had been seen on the track. He asked what he was doing. James explained the situation, saying he had merely stopped to keep the old man company while he waited for a friend to help him with his pack up the hill. Without hesitation Sula offered to do that. If James didn't want him for any particular reason he would be going that way home. He picked up the pack, and with that they parted, James putting his best foot forward to make up for lost time, Sula and the old man, profuse in his thanks, proceeding in the opposite direction. The last James saw of them they were walking up the hill together.

At this juncture James had not the remotest suspicion that there might be anything wrong in this; that the story the old man had told was anything but the truth. There was no reason why he should be suspicious. There was nothing extraordinary in the old man's behaviour, unless it was, perhaps, his obvious attempt to detain him. By the time he reached home he had dismissed the incident from his mind.

He arrived to see a man mounting a horse that had been tethered at the gate. He perceived from his uniform that he was a policeman, or one of the special "runners" who acted for them. In passing he asked if there was anything wrong.

The runner said there was nothing wrong, but he had been sent to warn the *sahib*—meaning James' father—to let it be known there might be a Thug in the district. He had murdered a woman in the valley and was last seen walking in this direction. James said that in the absence of his father he was sure Lalu Din, who had charge of the office, would do all that was necessary. The runner went on his way and James entered the house, where, after a wash, he sat down to his lunch. The apprehension of a Thug being nothing to do with him he was prepared to forget the affair.

Had he been asked when the first glimmering of a suspicion entered his head he would not have been able to answer. He was not even thinking—at any rate, not consciously—of the stranger he had seen on the hill track. But suddenly he found himself pondering. Could it be possible that he had seen and spoken to the murderer? The possibility having taken root his brain began to race and he remembered details. The dark skin . . . the unfamiliar accent . . . the ingratiating manner . . . the way he was going, heading for the forest and the mountains, for no apparent purpose . . .

James rang the bell on the table. To the servant who answered he said: "Ask Lalu Din to speak to me."

Presently Lalu Din came. James asked him if he had spoken to the police runner. Lalu Din said yes, he had. They had talked while he had given him some refreshment.

"This Thug," said James. "Was the runner able to give a description of him?"

"No. He looked like any other beggar, except that he had very dark skin, and it was known that he had the scar of an old knife wound on his chin."

"Thank you," James said, and Lalu Din withdrew, leaving James with a sinking feeling in the stomach as he remembered he had last seen his friend, Sula Dowla, walking towards the forest with a stranger who had a dark skin and a scar on his chin. His appetite gone James thought fast; and the more he thought the more he became convinced that the man he had seen on the hill was the one for whom the police were looking. His pose of amiability; the way the old man had hinted that in the absence of his friend he might help him up the hill. Had that been a trick to get him into the forest? Had there been a gleam in the man's eyes when he had made this proposal—or was it imagination in view of what he now knew? Sula had gone with him —towards the forest.

Suddenly James made up his mind. There was only one thing to be done if he was not to have a sleepless night wondering if Sula was all right . . . safe and sound . . . or . . . He dare not think of the alternative. There might still be time to save him. He knew that the usual Thug method was to wait until after dark before strangling their victim; if possible when he was asleep.

If it is thought that James was unduly upset it must be remembered that for a boy he led a rather lonely life. There was no other British boy of his age near his home, so it was almost inevitable that for a companion he should sometimes turn to one of the Indian boys he knew. Such a one was Sula Dowla. He liked Sula and they had more than once shared danger.

One thing that puzzled him, and gave him hope, was this. Why should a Thug murder him? He possessed nothing of value. Certainly no money. Even his clothes were not worth stealing, consisting as they did of nothing more than a loin-cloth held up by an old leather strap from which hung a small, cheap, very ordinary knife, an almost indispensable article for the sort of life he lived. His footgear was an old pair of tennis shoes which James had given him, and of these he was proud. But they had no market value.

But then James remembered that to Thugs wealth was of secondary importance. They killed for the sheer lust of killing, and they were not particular about a victim as long as they had one.

In the forest it would be a simple matter to strangle
Sula and dispose of his body where it was unlikely
ever to be found. Scavengers would soon leave no
trace of it. James went cold at the thought.

He told the servants he was going for a walk and
that he might be out for some time; but he didn't
say where he was going. This, as he was later to
realize, was a mistake, and he was to regret it. He
went to the gunroom, took his light rifle from its
rack, put some cartridges in his pocket and set off.
All of which was not very wise; but he was acting on
impulse without taking into account the possible
consequences of what he was doing. He was not so
much concerned with the Thug as the horrid thought
of what might happen to Sula if he failed to reach
him in time.

Again, it may be wondered why he didn't tell
Lalu Din, or some of the house servants, where he
was going and what he intended to do; which would
have been a sensible precaution. But it must be
remembered that he was still only acting on
suspicion and he hesitated to make himself look
foolish by starting what might turn out to be a false
alarm. Aside from that, Lalu Din, who was supposed to be responsible for him during his father's
absence, might forbid him to go out. True, he was
not likely to use force to restrain him; but there would
be an argument, and to defy the trustworthy and
conscientious servant would be unfair to him. He
would only be doing what he had been told to do;
carrying out his orders to the best of his ability. In

any case, let us admit it, James had not yet reached the years of discretion.

He set off up the hill track at his best pace, for the day now being far advanced he had no time to lose. Reaching the tea plantation where Sula lived with his parents he went straight to the bungalow and asked if he was at home. Sula's mother told him no, he had gone out that morning and had not yet returned. She was not worried; but then, as far as she knew, she had no reason to be. Sula usually was out. On hearing this news James' stomach seemed to sink a little lower. It was what he had dreaded to hear, for it looked as if his worst fears were likely to be realized.

On his way back to the road, such as it was, he saw one of the women who had been working going home. James asked her if she had seen Sula, whom of course she would know. She answered that she had seen him but it was some time ago. He had then been walking up the hill towards the forest with two men, strangers to her. James' stomach dropped still lower. But he wondered. Two men? Did that make Sula safe? Then, as they say of the automatic machines, the penny dropped. The Thug had been joined by the friend he had mentioned. He would certainly be another Thug. That meant there were now two of them. There was nothing surprising in that because James knew they often worked in pairs.

Now cold with apprehension he strode on up the hill towards the forest more than ever determined to find Sula; or, failing that, demand an explanation from the Thugs if he could overtake them.

There was this about the situation: Sula, dead or alive, must be somewhere in front of him because there was only a single track, so should he return he could not fail to meet him. Of course, he hoped this would still happen. It was all he needed to put his mind at rest.

Still travelling uphill he came to the jungle that fringed the forest proper. He knew this was a dangerous place where anything could happen, and for the first time he found himself regretting that he had not left word of where he was going. But it was too late to think about that now and he held on his way purposefully. So he came to the forest, still without seeing a sign of Sula.

The sun was now well down, and already under the great trees a dim green twilight had fallen. He was now both hot and tired and he had to consider how much farther he would be able to go before he became exhausted. He did not relish the idea of being benighted in the forest. Already it was an eerie place, full of strange sounds and stealthy rustlings, both on the ground and in the trees, as nocturnal creatures left their lairs in their nightly search for food.

But the thought that spurred him on was the certain knowledge that Sula must be somewhere in front of him. More than ever he now feared the worst. Why Sula had gone so far into the forest with two strangers he could not imagine. But then Sula was like that. He would have gone anywhere with anybody who wanted to be friendly.

James went on a little way and then, with the twilight deepening, hesitated. He had not expected to come as far as this. Doubts arose. What if the Thugs did not stop, but went on to the high hills where they would be safe? The obvious danger, that they might ambush him and murder him, did not occur to him. He knew he was doing wrong; that if his father ever heard of this exploit he would be very angry. Another thought that made him feel uncomfortable, and even ashamed, was the knowledge of the hue and cry that would be started to search for him if he failed to return home before dark. Poor old Lalu Din would be in a panic. It wasn't fair to him.

Only once had James been up the track as far as this and on that occasion he had not been alone. He had been in the care of an experienced officer of the Forest Service whose purpose it had been to inspect a damaged *dak* bungalow (rest-house) to see if it was worth repairing. That was some time ago, and he did not know if the old wooden building had been put in order or demolished. As far as he could remember the place was about half a mile ahead. He thought the Thugs might be making for it as a place to pass the night. He felt sure they would not be too keen on travelling after dark. What became of the track after that point he did not know.

After giving the matter some consideration he decided to go on as far as the *dak* bungalow, or the site of it, to see if it was still there. If it was, should

he find it unoccupied he would return home forth-
with and report his suspicions, feeling he had done
as much as was reasonable. He realized that to go
alone beyond that point would be the limit of folly.
If the Thugs had not stopped there they might by
this time be in the mountains. His final resolution
was this. If the Thugs were there alone, and this he
thought he should be able to ascertain by careful
scouting, they could remain unmolested as far as he
was concerned; but if they had Sula with them he
would have to tell him who his companions were
and see him safely home. He no longer had any
doubts about the man he had seen, and spoken to,
on the road being the man who had murdered the
woman in the valley; for he could think of no possible
reason why a normal Indian should come as far as
this into the forest at such an hour. Indians knew
the risks even better than he did.

His mind made up he went on, eyes and ears very
much alert, for let it not be supposed that he was
happy about the situation in which he had put himself. He knew he was asking for trouble. If the
truth must be told, in his fast-beating heart he was
regretting that he had started on such a foolhardy
enterprise, for that, really, was what it was; and he
was intelligent enough to know it. But the thought of
Sula, unconscious of his danger, was the magnet that
drew him on. If it was learned later that he had
been murdered the knowledge that he had abandoned him to his fate would haunt him all his life.
No. Anything rather than that.

He reached his objective, the *dak* bungalow, without incident. There was still just enough light for him to see the clearing. Approaching with extreme caution he saw the dilapidated building was still there. A faint flicker of firelight came from the window. From inside, the murmur of voices. That told him all he needed to know. Someone was there. It could only be the Thugs. It couldn't be anyone else. But the big question remained to be answered. Was Sula with them? He listened, hoping to hear his voice, for that would at least tell him he was still alive. That was all that mattered.

James' rifle was already loaded. He slipped off the safety catch with his thumb to be ready for instant action and step by step advanced to the window. One quick peep was enough. Sula was there, sitting cross-legged on the floor, Indian fashion, between two men. A pack lay on the wooden boards beside them. In front of them a small fire of twigs was burning, presumably to make smoke to deter insects. It gave just enough light for James to identify the man, the man with the scarred face, who had accosted him that morning on the hill. The other man looked younger, more agile. Sula was laughing at something that had just been said, obviously unaware of the danger he was in. Of course, James still had no definite proof that these men were Thugs. Many Indians could show scars of old wounds. It may have been instinct but something told him he was right. These men were Thugs.

His first feeling was one of immense relief that he

had arrived in time. That Sula was still alive. This was followed by wonderment that Sula should have been so stupid as to travel so far into the forest with two strangers. But then, as we have said, he was not of a suspicious nature. He would no more imagine that his companions were Thugs than had James when he had sat beside the old man on the hill that morning. Moreover, Sula knew his way about. He had been born in the district. He lived there. He was wise to all the common dangers. But Thugs were not common. It was unlikely that he had ever seen one. He would not be thinking of the possibility of being murdered for no reason whatever.

James worked his way silently to the door. It stood ajar. In fact, as it was hanging on one hinge it could not be shut. With his rifle at the ready he pushed it wide open with a foot, took a pace inside, poised, prepared to move fast. Instantly the talking ceased, ended as abruptly as a radio switched off. Three pairs of eyes flashed to him, staring. Not the least surprised of the three on the floor was Sula. His astonishment at seeing James at such a place was understandable. His eyes saucered. His amazement was revealed by the way he gasped James' name. "What—what are you doing here?" he stammered.

James spoke sternly and clearly although his heart was pounding. "Sula, come with me," he ordered.

"But why?"

"Don't argue. Come. I have reason to suspect these men are Thugs."

Sula's expression changed. He sprang to his feet, as did his companions, uttering cries of protest and abuse.

James kept them covered. Not for a second did he take his eyes off them. "Silence!" he commanded crisply. When the order was obeyed he went on: "You say you are not Thugs?"

"We are not Thugs," shouted the two men together.

"You have killed a woman in the valley."

"We have not been in the valley! We have not touched a woman!"

"We will see," retorted James, grimly. "Sula, cut open that pack."

More cries of protest from the men.

"If either of you move I will shoot," threatened James, speaking as if he meant it. Knowing his own life was now at stake he did mean it.

Sula opened the pack and began to drag out the contents. The first thing to appear was a woman's dress, a *sari*, torn and bloodstained, as if the owner had died struggling. As Sula held it up, from the folds fell three of the fine gold wire bracelets commonly worn by Indian women, who do not care much for artificial jewellery.

"If you have not touched a woman how did you get these things?" demanded James, although he knew the answer. This was the property of the murdered woman.

With that, hissing like a snake, the younger of the two Thugs sprang, one arm raised high, holding a curved dagger which he had snatched from his rags. James' rifle blazed. He did not take aim. There was no time for that. Instinctively he pointed the weapon and pulled the trigger. Sparks ended at the man's shoulder. The dagger flew out of his hand and he fell screaming on the floor where he rolled about, groaning. The older man, his eyes gleaming with fanatical hate, was groping under his ragged garments.

James jerked another cartridge into the breech. "Draw that knife and you die," he warned with iron in his voice.

There was a moment of brittle silence except for the groans of the man on the floor, now clutching at his shoulder where apparently he had been hit. James' brain was racing. Speaking to Sula he went on: "Run home and fetch your father, and men with ropes to tie up these Thugs."

"But you——"

"I shall stay here to see they do not run away. Do as I order. Go!"

Sula dashed out of the door to disappear into the night.

James regarded his two prisoners with cold hostility. He was beginning to tremble from shock but he kept himself under control knowing his life depended on it. The old man lay muttering incoherently. The other, still groaning, lay in a corner trying to stem the flow of blood now running

down his arm. James did nothing to help him,
realizing that to go near him would be madness.
Anyway, to admit the truth, at that moment he
didn't care if the man died. He was a murderer and
deserved to die, he thought.

The next hour seemed the longest he had ever
had to endure. The strain of standing there, watching for the slightest movement, muscles braced,
became almost unbearable. Not for an instant did
he dare to relax his vigilance, knowing what the
price of weakness would be. The old man, he knew,
had a knife, and given half a chance would not
hesitate to use it. No doubt he knew how to throw
it. His fanatical, ghoulish eyes blazed unwinkingly
at James. Twice he made a slight movement, but
froze with a snarl like a wild animal as James' rifle
lined up on him.

The ordeal ended, to James' unspeakable relief,
with a tumult of shouting rapidly approaching.
Then men poured into the room, not only Sula's
father with workers from the plantations but Lalu
Din and some of the house staff. It turned out
he had been looking for James, and hearing the
noise on the hill had joined the rescue party. Sula
was there, too, of course. He stood close to James,
touching him and muttering his thanks.

The two Thugs were trussed up like chickens
ready for market and dragged away to await the
arrival of the police, for whom a runner had already
been sent. James never saw them again.

As they plodded homewards Lalu Din said in a

voice heavy with reproach: "O master, what will the *sahib* say to me when he hears of this?"

To which James answered, sadly: "What he will say to you, O Lalu Din, I do not know, but I can guess what he will say to me."

THE BLACK INTRUDER

HUNTERS and naturalists have long argued about the panther. Some aver that the leopard and the panther are one and the same creature. Certainly they are very much alike both in appearance and in habits. The truth may be that the animal varies slightly in different countries. The "rosettes", or spots, may vary in pattern. The Indian leopard is larger than the African. It may weigh up to 200 lbs. The Indian panther may not weigh quite as much as the leopard. It is certain they can have the same murderous qualities when they go "bad". One thing the panther can do, which its larger carnivorous cousins, the lions and tigers, cannot do, is run up a tree like a house cat. This enables it to catch monkeys. And the monkeys know it.

It is largely nocturnal. Normally it is shy and retiring, lying up in dense shade during the heat of the day. Yet, curiously enough, it is not afraid of man, and will often take up residence near a village. He is an expert at hiding himself and will take cover in a patch of grass apparently too small to conceal anything of his size. He can be bold to the point of recklessness. He probably possesses more cunning than his larger relations but he is just as fierce. Over a short distance he can run as fast as any creature on four legs. He does not roar like a lion or tiger, but when looking for a mate mews more like a cat. He is of course a flesh eater, preying chiefly on deer, goats, dogs and monkeys. He is particularly fond of dog, which may be why he will hang about a village, in the hope of pouncing on one. In India he can become a man-eater, and when he does he can become as much a curse as a man-eating tiger.

One famous man-eating leopard killed 125 people before he was slain. Another, in the Mandali district, killed 30 men and mauled many more. This sort of menace is not uncommon. The beast is difficult to kill because, as he can climb trees, it is not safe to wait for him in a *machan*—a platform in a tree.

Another animal about which there has been much argument is the *black* panther. At one time this, too, was thought to be a separate species, but it is now generally accepted that it is merely a case of melanism (black coloration) which can happen to other animals.

There may not be a more ferocious-looking animal in the world than a black panther. If Satan has a counterpart on earth surely this is it. There is one in the London Zoo. If ever you are there have a good look at it. Catch those hate-filled eyes and notice the way he flattens his ears and lifts a lip in a snarl to show those gleaming white fangs. He as good as tells you that were it not for those iron bars he would tear you to pieces and love to do it. He is found in tropical America as well as in Asia. Unfortunately, unlike the lion, which kills only for food and is then satisfied, its smaller relation will kill wantonly, regardless of whether or not it is hungry. Hence its unpopularity.

Oddly enough, many big game hunters in India who have killed tigers have never seen a panther, even the ordinary spotted type, although it is not uncommon. It has a trick of not being where one might be expected, but will turn up in a most unlikely place. Perhaps for that reason James had never seen one; wherefore he gave little thought to them. Certainly he never went out deliberately to look for one. He had no such ambition. On the contrary, he took care to keep well away from any place where one had been reported. Killing a panther was work for an experienced *shikari*, not for him.

As far as he knew, only one had been killed recently in the district. There was much talk of it at the time because it died in unusual circumstances. It seemed that two men, brothers, had gone out to cut firewood, for which purpose one carried an axe. Suddenly, for no reason at all, a panther sprang from a bush and seizing one of the men dragged him down. Whereupon the other, who happened to be the one carrying the axe, with great courage leapt to the rescue. Swinging the axe he brought it down on the panther's head, splitting it open and killing it on the spot; a feat which excited James' admiration although he had no desire to try to emulate it. His father had often told him that big game hunting was not for small boys.

Yet it was probably only a matter of time before a panther crossed his path, and this is how it happened.

He was lounging in the garden when he saw Habu Din going out. He carried a plaited wickerwork basket. The conversation that followed was a natural one between two boys. James said: "Where are you going?"

Habu replied: "I'm going to get some honey."

James smiled. He had once seen Habu with a jar of wild honey, an unholy mixture of syrup and wax mixed with dead bees, like a currant cake. Habu's method of eating it was to stick in a finger and suck it. He invited James to try it. He did, and found it excellent. As Habu proudly claimed, you could taste the flowers in it. This way of eating sweets may not be to everyone's taste, but it must be remembered that if Habu wanted something sweet there was little choice. There was no shop just round the corner, as in Europe, with shelves piled high with toffees, candies, chocolates and other delicacies dear to the boyish heart.

James said: "Where are you going to get the honey?"

"In the *bharbar*." (This is the belt of jungle that divides the plains from the high ground.)

"How are you going to find it?" inquired James.

"I know where some is."

"How do you know?"

"I've marked down a bees' nest."

"How did you manage that?"

Habu smiled knowingly. "I'm an Indian boy. I know how."

"Tell me."

"It's easy."

"How?"

"All you have to do is catch a bee."

"Then what?"

"You put a spot of gum on its back. On that you stick a little piece of feather."

"What for?"

"So you can see it and watch which way it goes back home."

"You mean you let the bee go?"

"Of course. All you have to do is follow it."

"How do you get the honey out of the nest?"

"Scoop it out with my hand."

"Don't you get stung?"

"Not much. I light a fire under the tree. The smoke stupefies the bees. If I get stung I don't mind. The honey is worth a few stings."

"Where exactly is this nest?"

"In an old tree."

"What sort of tree?"

"Mulberry. Why don't you come? You can have some of the honey."

James looked doubtful. "Bears like mulberries."

"They don't come so far down. There are better mulberries higher up, where they are."

"Bears also like honey."

"I've never seen a bear where I'm going, and I've been often."

"There could be all sorts of things in the *bharbar*."

"Nothing to hurt. It's not far past the plantations, where men will be working."

James began to weaken. "How far past the plantations?"

"A mile. Perhaps a little more."

James looked suspicious. He knew Habu's notion of a mile. "It's dangerous," he said.

"Of course, if you're afraid——"

"I'm not afraid," protested James hotly.

"If you're not afraid why don't you come?"

Of course, that did it. "I'll bring my rifle," James said.

"If you like, but you won't need it."

"Does your father know where you're going?"

"No. There's no need to tell him. He knows I can take care of myself."

"I'm not so sure of that," returned James. "But I'll come with you. Wait till I get my rifle."

In five minutes the boys were on their way, and in rather more than an hour they were on the fringe of the *bharbar*, here a mixture of jungle and forest, James not in the least surprised that Habu's idea of a mile was well short of the actual distance.

"This way," said Habu, taking the lead.

Not sharing Habu's confidence that they were not likely to encounter anything dangerous James loaded his rifle before entering that mysterious world where nature, animal and vegetable, works unimpeded by the strange things that men do, in freedom and in harmony; where there comes a feeling

E

that time has stood still for centuries. Of course the forest teemed with life. Birds called and twittered; monkeys chattered as they gambolled in the trees.

Habu seemed to know exactly where he was going, but from time to time, from force of habit, he stopped to listen for any sound that might indicate danger. In this way they reached the area of mulberry trees that was their destination. There were several, forming a group in a fairly open glade, broken here and there by tussocks of tall grass and patches of straggling *lantana* scrub.

Almost at once they came upon something that brought James to a halt. On the ground lay a gory mess of blood and beautiful feathers that had once been a peacock.

"What killed it, I wonder?" James said frowning.

"It doesn't matter."

"The blood's still wet. The bird hasn't long been dead."

"Forget it," Habu said impatiently. "Something is always killing something. Help me to collect grass to make smoke."

"Which is the tree?"

"That one." Habu pointed to a great old tree that must have stood there for centuries. But its days were nearly done. Half of it was dead. About twenty feet up a branch, torn from the trunk but not quite severed, hung to the ground to form an easy means of ascent. The scar showed that it was rotten. There was a large hole at the junction of the branch and the trunk around which bees were buzzing.

"We'll soon have the honey," declared Habu, putting down the basket and the jar that was to hold the spoils.

Suddenly something happened. A hush fell. Not a sound. As at a given signal the monkeys and the birds fell silent, as if stricken dumb. It was all the more striking after the incessant babble of sound to which their ears were now attuned. James froze to a statue, his eyes on Habu's face. Habu, too, stood stock still. An explanation was unnecessary. Both knew the signs.

James spoke in a whisper. "There's something here."

Habu did not answer. His attitude was tense, eyes alert, restless.

"There it goes," James said tersely, as a dark shadow flashed from one patch of *lantana* to another.

"A porcupine," Habu said, with a sigh of relief.

"No. It wasn't tall enough."

"A hyena."

"It wasn't the shape of any hyena I've seen."

"It must have been a jackal."

"It was too big for a jackal."

"It wasn't a tiger," Habu said hopefully.

"Of course it wasn't. Any fool can tell a tiger."

"Then what could it be?"

"I don't know."

It is no matter for wonder that the boys were puzzled. Even when James got his first clear view of the animal it took him a second to realize what it was.

James went on, still speaking in a whisper as if in a church. "I don't like this. Don't forget that peacock we saw. Don't you think we'd better go?"

"Not till I've got some honey," Habu said obstinately, and without waiting for James to protest started walking towards the old tree plucking grass as he went. James did not move. He was still staring at where he had last seen the shadow.

Then it happened. The air was rent with a piercing shriek; the sound that comes when death strikes. It was hard to say just where it came from. In the treetops a troop of monkeys screamed together. Again silence fell: a solemn hush more nerve-chilling than the noise. James' thumb slid up the rifle and took off the safety catch.

"A hyena," Habu said. But there was no confidence in his voice.

"You know better than that," replied James shortly. "Don't fool yourself, Habu. Something has killed a monkey. A hyena couldn't catch a monkey."

"A leopard, perhaps. Leopards catch monkeys."

"What I saw didn't look like a leopard to me," declared James. "It was too dark. I'm sure there were no spots on it. There's a killer here. Let's go."

"If it has caught a monkey it won't bother with us, whatever it is," stated Habu, more in hope, James thought, than confidence.

The boys stood still, hesitant, looking, listening, every nerve taut, for two or three minutes. They saw nothing. They heard nothing.

Habu said: "It's gone!"

"I wouldn't be too sure of that, but I sincerely hope you're right," answered James grimly. "I'm going, too. I've had enough of this."

They began to walk away. Instantly from somewhere near came a low, rasping snarl.

Dropping the grass he had plucked Habu went up the fallen branch like a monkey.

James stood his ground. He knew it was the best thing to do. The only movement he made, and he made it slowly, was to bring his rifle half-way to the shoulder, finger on the trigger. He knew that a sudden movement was almost certain to provoke a charge.

Nothing happened.

Beginning to breathe more freely he said to Habu: "You can please yourself what you do but I'm going home."

"Wait for me, I'm being stung," pleaded Habu from a perch in the tree, and returned to earth via the fallen branch.

James continued walking. But not for long. He had taken only two or three paces when from a tussock of grass that looked too small to hold anything larger than a hare sprang an animal that must have been stalking them. It was black. Jet black. Against which its teeth gleamed like ivory. From its size and shape James knew it could only be one thing. A panther. That rare creature, a black panther. For some reason known only to itself, but possibly because he was standing still, it ignored James. Habu, on the other hand, was on his way back to the tree, and he was losing no time on the way. Reaching it with a yard or two to spare he went up it like a jack-in-the-box.

Seeing what was likely to happen James snapped a shot at the panther; but, low on the ground, it was travelling like a black arrow and he did not make sufficient allowance. From the way it growled and bit at its foot he judged he had struck one of its hind paws. But this did not stop it. It went on up the tree after Habu.

All this happened in a matter of seconds. Habu was now well on his way to the top of the tree, apparently forgetting that he was being pursued by an expert at the business. But, of course, there was no other way for him to go. He screamed when he saw the panther coming up after him. James' fear now was that he would fall. Having reloaded he fired again, this time more carefully, at the black shape spread-eagled against the trunk of the tree as it went on up. He heard the bullet thud home.

The panther stopped. It turned its head and looked round, and down, and James was never to forget the expression of demoniac hate in the eyes that glared down at him. The face was twisted into a hideous mask as the great cat spat at him. Then it tried to climb, but failed. It began to slide, slowly at first, but faster as the weakening claws lost their grip on the bark. It fell the last few yards, tore up the earth for a moment or two and lay still.

James had reloaded. He was taking no chances. His *shikari* friend, the Skipper, had told him: "Always one more shot before you go close to a dangerous beast which you think is dead. Always one more shot to make sure. To forget that is asking to be mauled."

Taking his time James put another bullet into what was now a stationary object. It was an easy shot. The panther did not move. He advanced cautiously and put another bullet behind the ear into the brain. Then he looked up at Habu, and in a voice that he hardly recognized as his own, he called: "It's all right. You can come down now."

Habu came shakily down the tree, smiling sheepishly when he reached the ground. For some seconds the two boys stood looking at the dead animal.

"I seem to remember you saying there was nothing here likely to hurt us," reminded James coldly. "What about this?"

Habu made a gesture. "It is true. But I have never seen anything like this here. Who could have expected it? It must have come from far away."

James contemplated the panther, a picture of feline perfection. "What a beautiful creature," he said sadly. "Pity I had to shoot it."

Habu obviously did not share these sentiments. "The son of Satan is better dead," he declared. "The monkeys and everything else here will be happy. You made a good shot. Thank you."

"Lucky for you I brought the rifle," James said. "Do you still want to get some honey?" he added, looking around. "This fine fellow may have a mate near."

Habu smiled wanly. "I seem to have lost my taste for honey. I think I'll go home."

"I'll come with you," returned James. "On the way we'll call at the plantation and tell the men what lies here. One of them might like the skin. It seems a pity to let it lie here to rot."

"Don't you want it?"

"Me? No. It would give me a fright every time I looked at it."

Habu Din smiled.

They set off for home.

A PROFESSOR LEARNS A LESSON

JAMES had never been up to the really high ground, the upper foothills of the Himalayas, that lay to the north of Mirapore where his father was stationed. This itself was at the northern tip of the United Provinces, near Garhwal. One reason may have been that he never had a reason to go. It would have been a long and arduous journey, anyway. It is unlikely that he would ever have gone had it not been for an unusual circumstance. Even then he had no definite purpose, and in the ordinary way it is unlikely that his father would have allowed him to go; but it had been an exceptionally hot spell of weather, and everyone, natives as well as Europeans, was feeling the strain. That was another reason why the trip ever took place. It was thought the cool mountain air would be beneficial to his health, which in the torrid heat had not been too good. It turned out to be a memorable experience, not without educational value.

The adventure began, although James was not to know it at the time, with the arrival at the house of a horse and cart of the type often used locally for longish journeys where there was no other means of transport. In the cart were two men and a load of luggage. James knew one of the men. It was his *shikari* friend, Captain Lovell, whom he knew well enough to call 'Skipper'.

The other was a stranger, a young man in the early twenties, immaculate in obviously new white ducks and extra large pith helmet; and from the colour of his skin James judged he had not been in India for very long. This turned out to be correct. It had not had time to become tanned by the sun. Indeed, as it was learned later, this was his first visit to the tropics.

It turned out that he had come on a curious mission. Or at least so it seemed to James when he learned what it was. By local standards it was certainly unusual. Captain Lovell explained it that evening, James' father having provided accommodation for them in the house, their stay being a short one.

The stranger had been introduced as Professor Nigel Desmond, an American, and the Skipper was acting as his guide and escort. He was tall, thin, with a high forehead from which the hair was already beginning to recede. He wore large spectacles. Naturally, he spoke with an American accent. James thought he seemed a nice enough fellow, if inclined to talk with too much self-assurance about matters of which he could have had no practical experience. Later, at the first opportunity they had to speak alone, the Skipper confirmed this opinion by saying he thought the Professor's knowledge had been acquired from books. However, James thought none the worse of him for that. As the Skipper remarked, everyone had to learn.

To make a long story as short as possible, it transpired that Professor Desmond was a biologist and a naturalist of repute, with several letters after his name which meant nothing to James. He took them to be university degrees, and at least they sounded impressive. He was also, it seemed, a taxidermist, as he would have to be for what he intended to do.

He was now working for an important natural history museum in America. It was a new one and anxious to extend its exhibits. He admitted that he was at a disadvantage in not knowing a word of any Indian language, wherefore the Skipper had been engaged to make the necessary arrangements for him, to help him to get to his proposed destination. This was the hill country to the north of Garhwal. As he might be there for some time the Skipper would have to leave him to make his own way home.

The main purpose of the Professor's expedition was to secure specimens of those difficult animals, the goral, the tahr, and, if possible, a markhor. They were difficult in that they were extremely shy, and living among crags were not easy to approach. They were not in any way dangerous. He had brought with him everything he was likely to require for obtaining the skins, for their preservation and shipment home, when they would be stuffed, mounted, and put on exhibition in the museum.

It seemed to James that he had also brought a lot of things he would not require, at least by normal standards. James had never seen so much equipment. A tent, a rifle, camera, medicine, a chest of rupees to pay his bearers, these things he could understand, but others, such as a portable bath and a quantity of luxury foodstuffs, seemed quite unnecessary. They would all have to be carried, and that would mean a lot of porters. It was evident that the Professor had been to some pains to avoid anything like discomfort.

There was nothing wrong with this, of course, but to James it was something new. All the white hunters he had known, and he had known several, believed in 'travelling light', not necessarily because they could not afford expensive equipment but because it was the thing to do. They preferred their sport the hard way. A lot of luggage could be a nuisance, anyway.

However, James made allowances for the fact that the Professor was not concerned with sport. The expedition had a scientific purpose, and apparently money was no object. At first, when the Professor referred to animals like goral, tahr and markhor, James was at a loss to know what he was talking about. He had never even heard of these creatures, much less seen one. But this was understandable because they did not occur in any part of India that he knew; consequently they were never discussed.

The Professor, who seemed to know all about

them, explained, somewhat condescendingly James thought, considering he could never have seen one of these animals either. However, he tried not to be too critical of a stranger. It was just his manner. No doubt he meant well.

The goral was the native name for a horned animal related to antelopes and goats. It had thick, coarse, dark hair to protect it from the cold in the region where it lived. The tahr was also a wild goat. The markhor was similar, with spiral horns. They were all mountain dwellers and remarkable for the speed at which they could run up apparently unscalable crags, where it might be thought nothing on legs could find a foothold. They had been hunted for generations by the hill tribesmen who had to live on what the country could provide. This had made them so wary that they were now very difficult to approach; but the hill-men had devised their own method of trapping them, as the travellers were to discover.

Professor Desmond remarked casually that he was also hoping to get an *ounce*, an animal about the size of a leopard with a pale yellowish-grey coat and a short thick mane sometimes known as the snow leopard. James knew something about these because he had seen their skins offered for sale in the bazaar at Allahabad. Not many people had seen a live one; it was so rare and so timid that one had never been known to attack a man.

Just how the Professor hoped to get near these nervous and uncommon creatures he did not say.

James asked him if he had ever done any stalking. To his astonishment the Professor admitted that not only had he never stalked anything but he had never shot anything in his life. In fact, until just before he had started on this present undertaking he had never fired either a gun or a rifle. He had done some practice at a rifle range. James can be forgiven if he began to wonder how this was going to work out when it came to hard facts. So apparently did the Skipper from the way he glanced at James and raised an eyelid.

The Skipper then explained his part in the operation. He would take the horse and cart as far as it could go; that is to say, take a route to the hills where there were bridges suitable for wheeled vehicles over the several rivers they would have to cross, tributaries of the Ganges which rose in the mountains and watered the whole region. These bridges, like the track, had been built by the Forestry Service for the transport of timber. They had also established *dak* bungalows at intervals although few of these now had a resident caretaker. But that didn't matter. In this way he hoped to reach the village of Dardani in three days.

That was as far as the cart would be able to go. It would be left there, and from then on travel would be on foot with Garhwali porters carrying the luggage. These would be changed from village to village until the necessary altitude was reached. The Garhwalis or Kumaons whom they might meet were good porters, so there should be no difficulty about that. They would be glad to earn some money.

The Skipper estimated that it would take a week to get to the high ground where the animals the Professor wanted were to be found. There, the necessary arrangements for hunting having been made with the local people, he would leave the Professor and return home. The hunting might take some time and he wouldn't be able to wait. But by that time the Professor should know enough about the country to manage without any great difficulty.

"Without some knowledge of the language that might not be as simple as it sounds sitting here," James said.

"I'm afraid there's no alternative," said the Skipper. "I shall have to get back."

"What about me?" suggested James.

"What about you?"

"If the Professor wouldn't mind having me in the party I could be useful acting as interpreter. The Professor might have an accident, or be taken ill, then what would he do? On these trips, as you know, all sorts of things can happen," concluded James.

Now when he said this he did not expect to be taken seriously. He was fully prepared for his father to squash the proposal on the spot. But to his surprise he hesitated.

"That makes sense to me," said the Skipper. "Really, it would be better if he had with him someone who, in case of emergency, can speak the language."

"Yes, it would be a wise precaution," agreed James' father. "The boy needs a change from this sweltering heat. A breath of fresh mountain air should do him a power of good."

Professor Desmond looked dubious. "Is a boy of his age qualified for such a journey?"

The Skipper answered: "You needn't worry about that. If you knew as much about the country as he does you wouldn't need me for a guide."

"Is he safe with a firearm?" queried the Professor.

"If you can shoot as fast and as straight as he can you should have no difficulty in getting your goral."

"Okay, if you say so," returned the Professor. "If it suits you it suits me."

So, before the evening was over it was settled that James should make the third member of the party. He was delighted. This would be a new experience. He had always had a hankering to go to the mountains, which he could see but had not had a chance to reach.

The following morning saw the party on the road, travelling by horse and cart. The Skipper and the Professor sat in front. James sat behind on his luggage, a light valise which was in fact a sleeping bag. It contained his toilet things, the Professor having said he had enough food for everyone. Apart from the valise all James had with him was his rifle and cartridge bag. They made good time and evening found them on schedule at the first resthouse.

To narrate the rest of the journey in detail would be tiresome repetition. Dardani, the terminus of the cart track, was reached on the third day without any incident worth recording. To James this was easy travel, and with the air becoming cooler for every thousand feet of altitude he was enjoying every minute. He knew, of course, the hard part was yet to come.

At Dardani the horse and cart were left in charge of the headman, who made no trouble of finding the required number of porters. Loads were arranged, and early the following morning, under a clear blue sky, the march was resumed on foot. It was uphill work and heavy going but James still enjoyed it. He had never felt so fit and began to appreciate the difference altitude could make.

The air was so clear that it seemed to sparkle, and objects a long way off could be seen in wonderful detail. By the end of the fourth day the tropical forest was becoming thinner. In front of them towered the mountains for which they were making, their flanks heavily clothed in trackless forest of spruce and fir that stretched for hundreds of miles. Beyond, still in the distance, hung what appeared to be drifts of white cloud, but which James knew were the peaks of the mighty Himalayan giants, covered with eternal snow. The so-called Roof of the World.

The party did not stop for anything except an occasional rest, and the objective, a Garhwali village in a valley at 10,000 feet, was reached on the sixth day. The tent was pitched and camp made. James was tired, partly no doubt as a result of the rarefied atmosphere after the humid heat of the plains, but he tried not to show it. His outstanding memory of the first night was waking up chattering with cold; from which he realized they were in the frost area where, just before dawn, the temperature could drop to below freezing point. It did not occur to him that this might have a bearing on what the Professor intended to do. Presumably the Skipper didn't know, either, or he would have given a warning. In the morning he made the final arrangements and left for the long walk home.

As soon as he had gone Professor Desmond started to make certain arrangements of his own. One of them, harmless on the face of it and no doubt made with the best intentions, was to offer a reward of a hundred rupees for every skin obtained. He only wanted the skin. The village could have the meat. Of course, this delighted the hillmen, but James was not sure it was wise. It would have been better, he thought, to let them know this after the event, because they would now make certain that something was killed, no matter how, if necessary by employing their own methods. And they would have their own methods he was sure. That was how snow leopard skins came into the bazaar at

Allahabad, when white hunters almost invariably failed to catch sight of the beast.

The Professor's next move was to appear with a pair of high-magnification binoculars over his shoulder. James asked him what he was going to do. The Professor, pointing to a peak that rose behind the village, said he was going to the top of the hill to spy out the land. To which James replied he would have thought it better to leave that sort of thing to the men the Skipper had arranged to act as guides. They must know every inch of the ground. The Professor said, rather shortly, that he would prefer to use his own eyes. James said no more, but as he walked up the hill with the Professor he thought about the remark. He would have put his trust in the local hunters, who would know every crag, every stone, within miles. Their lives depended on it. They would know of conditions that might not be revealed even by binoculars. However, it was the Professor's expedition, not his, so it was not for him to argue. After a hard climb—harder, James thought, than the Professor had supposed—they reached the summit. There the Professor lay down and began his 'spy' in the approved manner, surveying thoroughly the crags around them. After some time he said in a low, excited voice: "I can see them."

"See what?"

"Goral."

"Where?"

"Over there to the right. There's a small herd, in

charge of what I take to be a fine male, on that plateau above the valley. Here, take the glasses."

James took the binoculars and saw that the Professor was right. The herd appeared to be grazing peacefully. He handed back the glasses.

"I'll tell you something else," went on the Professor. "If they stay where they are they should be easy to stalk. I can see what I take to be a goat track winding round the flank of the mountain. It ends just below the plateau. From there the animals should be within range."

James glanced at the sun, now well up. "It's a long way," he said dubiously. "I doubt if we could get there before dusk. I wouldn't care to try to get back along that track after dark; it looks dangerous to me even in daylight. Nor would I care to spend the night on the plateau. It would be freezing cold. We should have started earlier."

"That's all right," returned the Professor eagerly. "There's no great hurry. We can go tomorrow, starting at dawn. That should give us time to get there and back in daylight."

"The goral may not still be there."

"I think they will. I'd say they're on one of their regular feeding grounds. They are not likely to move far. We can keep an eye on them."

"We'll ask the headman for his opinion," James said. "The Skipper said he was wise. If in doubt ask him."

They went back down to the village where, finding the *mallik* (headman), by name Lal Das,

James reported what they had seen and explained what the Professor proposed to do.

To his surprise, for he could see nothing against the plan, the old man objected vehemently saying the track was dangerous. He did not say *why* it was dangerous and James would never have guessed. Nor would any stranger to the district. He merely said he knew of a better way to kill a goral, although, again, he did not say how. He agreed that the herd would probably be in the same place the next day. If they *must* go that way it would be better to go later.

James, now speaking in English of course, translated, telling the Professor of the old hunter's objections to the plan.

"Sure, sure," answered the Professor airily. "He's probably thinking of saving himself trouble. Or I guess maybe he's hoping to kill the goral himself to claim the reward."

"I'm sure he's thinking of saving *us* trouble," argued James.

"Well, I prefer to do things my own way. Don't take any notice of the old man. We don't need him with us. He's only an ignorant native."

This annoyed James. He bridled. "These people may be ignorant according to university standards but they know all there is to know about conditions where they live; and that's as much as they need to know for their own good, which is more than can be said for some white men," he retorted.

Apparently this annoyed the Professor. "Okay

—okay—but we'll do things my way," he said tartly. "If you don't like them you can go home. No doubt you can manage that."

There was a hint of a sneer in the last sentence, born, James suspected, of a sort of jealousy of his knowledge of the country and its people. He said no more, but he felt that if the Professor persisted in this attitude he was likely to end up in trouble. Even he, James, born in the country, was always prepared to accept the advice of local people. He told Lal Das that the Professor *sahib* had decided to go his own way to shoot a goral.

Upon which the old man threw up his hands and called upon God to witness that he had done his best to save trouble. And there the matter ended, leaving James disturbed in his mind for what the future might hold. However, there was nothing he could do about it.

The rest of the day was spent making preparations for the morning. The Professor made another trip, alone, to the top of the hill, and returned well pleased to report that the goral were still on the same plateau.

It was another bitterly cold night, and even in his sleeping bag James awoke frozen stiff. He was glad to get up to make the coffee.

The stars were still hanging like beacons in the sky when they moved off. James had looked for Lal Das but could not find him. He had gone out with some hunters, he was told. James thought this rather odd but put it down to the old man's determination to see that a goral was bagged—which in a way was true. No doubt the village was in need of meat.

The trail round the mountain, climbing ever higher, was a hard one, as James knew it would be, even without the old hunter's advice. In places it was a mere cornice, at the best a narrow ledge, worn by countless generations of mountain animals. It wound in and out a succession of gaunt, mostly barren slopes, sometimes with sheer cliff on one side and on the other a precipice that fell into a ravine, the bottom of which could not be seen, only the tops of the tangle of trees that filled it. There was a river there. James couldn't see it but he could sometimes hear it splashing its way to its distant parent, the Ganges. The sun had not yet topped the surrounding mountains and the thin air was still perishing cold, so he was glad of the exercise.

With the Professor striding along in front, rifle and binoculars slung over his shoulders, they reached a point which James reckoned to be about a third of the way to the objective although still well below it. It was a nasty, narrow place. The track could be seen ahead, winding on interminably as it seemed, in and out, up and down, on and on. It could not be seen all the time because there were places where it disappeared in clefts between flanks of the mountain; but it could usually be seen far in front as it rounded a distant *massif*.

It was here that the unexpected happened.

Looking at the track on the opposite side of a wall of rock, his near view being obscured by a similar formation, to his astonishment James saw an animal coming towards them. It was without doubt the beast they were seeking. A goral. And, moreover, it was a big male, with a fine spread of horns. It was galloping as if it had been frightened. The Professor saw it, too. Turning to James a smiling face he exclaimed: "What luck! Don't move. We can wait here for him to come to us. I'll drop him as he comes round the bend." The bend to which he referred was where the track re-emerged from a deep cleft in the rock. This was not more than sixty yards in front of them.

The Professor unslung his rifle, dropped on one knee and waited. James crouched behind him, expectant, hoping the Professor would allow the goral to get well round the corner before he fired, so that should he miss, and the animal turn back, there would be time for a second shot before he disappeared again round the bend. As for luck, he was not so sure about that. It was too lucky to be true. Why should the goral leave the herd? Why should it leave the plateau? There could be only one reason. It had been disturbed. Scared, by the speed at which it was moving. What could have alarmed it? The only thing it had to fear was man. What man? James thought he knew the answer. Lal Das. Or one of his hunters. So *that* was where he had gone. To the far side of the plateau. To drive the goral towards them and shorten their journey. If this was the scheme it looked as if it was going to succeed.

The goral was out of sight in the cleft, which must have been a deep one from the time it took to re-appear. Then it was there, coming round the bend, still at a gallop. The Professor took aim.

What happened next James would have found hard to describe. Without warning the animal began to behave as if it was wearing roller skates. It skidded, slithered and slid as if trying to stop, or turn. It struck the face of the rock, bounced off it, did a long slide and, unable to recover, dis-appeared over the edge of the precipice on the other side. A moment of silence and the crash could be heard as the heavy beast fell into the trees at the bottom of the ravine.

The Professor lowered his rifle and turned an astonished face to James. "Did you see that?" He laughed. "And I was told a goral had never been known to fall!"

"Well, this one did," was all James could say. Before he could go on to express his suspicions the Professor was running down the track to the spot where the goral had come to grief, presumably to see if it was possible to get down into the ravine to recover the body. James shouted to him to wait, but either the Professor did not hear or he took no notice.

James walked on, following slowly, pondering the remarkable thing he had seen. Could the goral have put a foot between two rocks and broken a leg? he

wondered. It seemed possible but unlikely. Then he
stopped dead, eyes wide with horror as what had
happened to the goral now happened to the Professor. He staggered, he tried to stop, he slid. He
clutched at the air in an effort to save himself, the
rifle flying out of his hands. A cry broke from his
lips, and to James' unspeakable horror he saw him
disappear into the chasm.

For a moment James could only stand there,
staring, stunned by the calamity and the speed at
which it had happened. He tried to think. What
could have caused it? Obviously something had;
something unusual. What could it be? Advancing
with extreme caution he saw the answer. Ice. But
not ordinary ice, such as ice that might have formed
on pools of stagnant water. It was in regular pieces
at definite intervals as if it had been put there by
design. It took him a minute or two to ascertain
exactly what it was. The ice was on mats. Native
woven mats. They were solid ice. How could they
have got there? James' racing brain told him they
must have been put there deliberately. But who
would do such a thing? Now he began to understand the headman's anxiety that they should not
use the track. He must have known about this.
Could he have been responsible? He found it
difficult to believe that.

A distant shout made him look up and he saw the
man himself, Lal Das, followed by some of his men,
running down the track where the goral had first
appeared. So that was the answer to the mystery.

He knew about this; that the place was a trap. James felt sick.

Later he was to learn the truth. That the local native method of trapping a goral was to put out mats soaked with water. During the night these froze to sheets of ice, loose sheets on the hard rock. Then the animals were stampeded. Running all unsuspecting on the ice they slipped and fell to their deaths. This may not be a sporting way of killing a wild animal, but the men who practised it were not interested in sport. Living where they did they needed meat in order to exist, and this was the easiest way of getting it. Cartridges, even if they could get them, were expensive. All this was explained to James later.

At the moment he didn't know what to do. There seemed to be nothing he could do. He was sure the Professor must be dead. His hands were trembling and his legs felt weak and shaky from shock. He sat down with his back to the rock face, to recover and wait for Lal Das and his men to arrive.

When they did they approached the trap with great care, picking up the mats as they came to them and stacking them in a heap. This, of course, made it evident that they knew about them, and their purpose.

When Lal Das came up to him James said coldly: "Did you do this?"

Lal Das answered cheerfully that he did. He wanted to be sure of killing a goral for the Professor *sahib*. "Where is he?" he asked, looking round.

James couldn't trust himself to speak. He simply pointed to the ravine.

The old man's cheerful expression faded. He threw up his hands in horror, again calling upon God to witness that he had tried to do his best to be helpful, that he had implored them not to use the track, or if they *had* to use it wait for the sun to rise— presumably to melt the ice—and so on and so on until James stopped him with an impatient gesture. He was sure the old man had acted with the best intentions. Naturally he would be anxious to see the Professor get his goral, for not only would he get some meat but be paid for it. The mistake of offering a reward was now apparent.

The old man stood silent, his head hung in shame and remorse, while it dawned on James that he, or someone, would have to go down the ravine to re-cover the Professor's body, and that was an urgent matter. He crawled to the edge of the ravine and looked down, but all he could see were the tops of the crowded trees. He was about to get up to ask Lal Das how they could get down when from far below came a faint cry for help. "He's alive—he's alive," he said unbelievingly. He shouted into the ravine: "Professor, are you all right?" It struck him as a silly thing to say but he could think of nothing else.

There was no answer.

"Professor, can you hear me?" yelled James.

The answer was a weak call that might have been "help".

James sprang to his feet and went into action, automatically taking command of the situation. "The Professor *sahib* is not dead," he told Lal Das in a voice tense with urgency. "We must get to him quickly. Which is the best way?"

The old hunter said it was impossible to get into the ravine from where they were. They would have to go back to the village and enter it from the end. He, too, realized the necessity for speed.

"Let us go," said James, picking up the Professor's rifle, and knowing it was loaded, unloaded it. Then again he knelt at the brink of the chasm. "Hold on," he shouted. "We are coming."

The return to the village was a race against time; but as James marched he was thinking, planning. By the time they arrived he had worked out what had to be done, and how to do it with the limited resources available. The thing that worried him most was his own shortcomings as a doctor. Even if the Professor was still alive by the time they were able to reach him he could not fail to be injured, probably seriously. Short of a miracle there would be broken bones. He would be too ill to be moved far, if at all. He would need a doctor. For this problem there was no immediate answer. There was no doctor; and small hope of getting one to the spot within at least ten days.

He was also worried by an uncomfortable feeling that in some way he might be held responsible for what had happened although he was satisfied

in his own mind that if anyone was to blame it was
the Professor himself, for ignoring the headman's
advice—indeed, his warning; for thinking that he
knew better than the local people; ignorant natives,
he had called them. It was really a case of too little
knowledge being a dangerous thing. James had
gone as far as he dare to point out the folly of
this; but in his position as the Professor's guest he
could not insist. He was only a boy without any
authority. Whatever the outcome of the tragedy he
could only hope that his father and the Skipper
would appreciate this. But he was anxious and
unhappy.

As soon as they arrived at the village the first
thing he did was to ask for the fastest runner who
was prepared to go to Mirapore. Lal Das produced
a man. James scribbled a brief note saying what
had happened and a doctor was needed with the
greatest urgency. This he gave to the runner, with
a handful of *rupees* from the Professor's money box,
and the man went off.

There was no time to make a stretcher; instead he
used the Professor's camp bed for the purpose.
However badly he was hurt he couldn't be left
lying in the jungle. Even if he was already dead
his body would have to be brought out. It couldn't
be left to become the prey of wild animals. So with
the bed, the Professor's medicine chest and a few
other things that might be needed, all carried by a
dozen stalwart Garhwalis under the leadership of
Lal Das, the rescue party set off, plunging straight

into the tangle of forest and jungle that followed the course of a mountain stream through the ravine. There was a path of sorts, probably a game track. James didn't know. He didn't care. He was concerned only with getting to the Professor. Lal Das knew every yard of the way and he was content to follow as the old man pushed on to the spot where the fall had occurred. From time to time they called. There was no answer.

James knew they had arrived when they came upon the goral. It was dead. Its neck was broken. Close by they found the Professor. He was alive but unconscious. There was a nasty wound on his forehead, still bleeding. From the angle of one of his legs it was obviously broken. That he was still alive was enough for James. He had fallen right through a tree and the branches must have broken his fall. He had brought some down with him. Fortunately the ground was a deep layer of soft leaf mould, and this, too, no doubt helped to save him from being killed instantly.

James could do nothing on the spot except wash and bandage the head wound. The thing to do, he decided, was to get him to the village while he was unconscious or the journey would be painful. He was lifted carefully on to his bed, and with three men carrying the goral, the return journey began. James felt better to know the Professor was alive although he still did not know how serious his injuries were. It may as well be said now, although this was not known until later, they included a broken leg, a dislocated shoulder, three broken ribs and numerous cuts and bruises.

Back in the village, in the tent, the women more or less took charge. They had had ample experience of accidental falls. They set the broken leg in splints, and as it turned out made a good job of it. Of course they knew nothing of the broken ribs.

Towards evening James was putting a fresh bandage on the Professor's forehead when he opened his eyes. His first words were: "Thanks. It was my own fault. I should have listened to you."

James admired him for that. Not every man is prepared to admit readily that he was wrong. He gave him a sleeping pill from the medicine cabinet as he was in considerable pain. The following day, after a fair night, he told him about the ice trap that had been the cause of the accident. He also cheered him by saying he had got the goral if not in the manner intended. He was attending to the preservation of the skin.

In the interval of waiting for the doctor to arrive he was able to improve on this by having the good luck to shoot a snow leopard. Lal Das told him he had seen one. They went after it and James shot it, really unwillingly, but he thought the knowledge that he had an *ounce* in the bag, as well as a goral, might compensate the Professor for what he was suffering.

Well, that is really the end of the story. The Professor recovered. It was nearly a fortnight

before a doctor arrived. With him came Captain
Lovell. He was still in the vicinity when the runner
had arrived at Mirapore. He told James that as
there was nothing more he could do he might as
well go home. Which he did.

He saw the Professor again, a month later, when
he arrived on a stretcher on his way to hospital for
final treatment. He was then a wiser man, as he
himself admitted after thanking James for his part
in the affair. He had seen to it that Lal Das and
his hunters were well rewarded for their efforts on
his behalf.

He would know better next time, he said with a
bleak smile.

F

THE FOOLISH TIGER

It may seem strange, considering that he lived in "tiger" country, that only once did James have to face a charging tiger. Or perhaps it is not so strange, because a normal tiger does not attack a man without a reason. It would rather avoid him, and in the majority of cases will do so. A confirmed man-eater is a different matter. This usually comes with advanced age, when a hungry tiger, with its strength failing, may find it easier to kill a human than the larger animals on which it usually preys. Having made the discovery this can become a habit. It may acquire a preference for human flesh. Or, of course, a tiger may be sick, or furious at having been injured, or wounded by a hunter.

James was not even thinking of tigers when he had to face one. Out for one of his constitutional walks, the day being fine, he had been up the hill to the tea estate for a gossip with Sula, a boy of his own age and the son of an Indian overseer. He took his rifle with him, more from force of habit than any expectation of having to use it. There had been no talk of a dangerous animal in the district, but one never knew when a defensive weapon might be needed.

He found Sula, and spent some time with him

talking about nothing in particular until his watch told him it was time to be returning home for lunch. Sula said he would walk part of the way with him. He would come as far as a place known as the Plains. This was not exactly a plain but a small piece of derelict open country that had once been under cultivation. Bounded by a strip of jungle it was now a flat waste of long grass with a certain amount of thin scrub. The local people commonly used it to collect grass for their domestic animals, goats and the like. Actually, the proper track skirted it, but to cross it offered a short cut, and James had used it regularly without the slightest trouble.

Having reached this point Sula had stopped, saying he would now turn back, when a woman, wild-eyed and with hair flying, rushed out of the grass shouting "Tiger—tiger". With hardly a glance at the boys she tore on without stopping.

"I'm going home," announced Sula, abruptly.

James smiled tolerantly. "Oh fiddlesticks! I bet it's a false alarm. She imagined it. What would a tiger be doing here? And if there is one it wouldn't be likely to interfere with us."

"I don't know," Sula said seriously. "That woman must have seen *something*. She looked pretty scared to me. See you tomorrow, perhaps." He made for home at a brisk pace looking anxiously to right and left.

With a shrug James continued on his way, taking the short cut, a matter of perhaps two hundred yards.

He had reached about halfway when he heard a low growl. It was hard to say exactly where it came from. He looked around, with his heart in his mouth as the saying is, for he knew that the growl could only have come from a tiger or a leopard. He stood still, common sense advising a return to the track. He was alarmed, but not really frightened, and it was only as a precautionary measure that he unslung his rifle, which was hanging on his shoulder. He still did not think he might have to use it, and he still had no intention of looking for trouble; but he slipped off the safety catch and waited for the sound to be repeated.

Then, as he stood there, hesitating, undecided whether to go on or turn back, a movement caught his eye, and he saw the face of a tiger rise slowly from the grass to stare at him. The animal was closer than he liked, not more than thirty yards away.

With his heart beating faster he stood absolutely still. He knew it was the only thing to do. More than once the Skipper had told him that to make a sudden movement, or to run away, was the most certain way to provoke a charge. His words came back to him: "Never run. That's fatal. You haven't a hope. Stand still and stare the beast out, and it may have second thoughts about coming for you."

This of course was sound advice, but in practice it was not as easy as it had sounded in theory. But James stood still and stared hard, hoping it would work. He thought it might. He knew that not all tigers are man-killers. The tiger stared back. These positions remained unchanged for what may have been a minute, although to James it seemed much longer than that. Then, by bad luck, something tickled the inside of his nose and he sneezed.

That did it. The tiger may have taken it for a challenge—but that was something only the tiger knew. With its eyes still on him it rose slowly to its feet. Its tail began to flick its sides. Now it will come, thought James, suddenly feeling surprisingly cool. Very slowly he brought the rifle to his shoulder and waited, still hoping the tiger would retire. It took two or three slow paces towards him. He noticed that it walked with a limp. Still hoping, he held his fire. It crouched, as if undecided.

Then it charged. Not in leaps and bounds, but in a low crouching run, as swift as the shadow of a cloud passing across the face of the sun. The matter no longer in doubt, James fired. The shot had no visible effect. He snapped in another cartridge and fired again. Still without effect. The tiger was now within ten yards. He just had time for one more shot, this time practically in the tiger's face, and that was it. He held out the rifle to take the impact of the blow he was sure would come.

Instead, an extraordinary thing happened. Something entirely unexpected. He was prepared to be knocked down and mauled, but he found himself still standing up. At the last instant the tiger seemed to swerve slightly and rushed past him, so close that he could have touched it. For a second his nose was filled with the strong smell of tiger. It did not stop. It ran straight on. James spun round on the ground on which he stood, at the same time reloading, sure that the tiger would come back. It did not turn. It ran on. James did not fire again. He watched the animal go on to the belt of jungle, into which, without a backward glance, it disappeared.

Still James did not move; unable to comprehend what had happened he waited, finger on trigger, his mouth dry from shock. Was the creature blind? he wondered. Was it a genuine charge or really an attempt to escape? Had his shots caused the animal to swerve at the last moment? That can happen. He didn't know the answer. He never did know. If it suited the tiger to go he was well content to let it go. He gave it five minutes. Once or twice he heard it growling in the bushes but it did not show itself. After it had been silent for a minute or two, with his eyes still on the jungle he began to move, without haste, towards the track. As he crossed the tiger's trail he saw spots of blood on the grass, which told him that at least one of his shots must have hit it.

Reaching the road, with a sigh of relief he looked back. There was no sign of the tiger. No sound. After a pause to steady himself he made for home, not without many a backward glance. He did not stop on the way. He had been severely shaken, and it would not be true to pretend otherwise. He walked into the garden to find his father there.

He was greeted by a long hard look. "I heard shots. Was that you?"

"Yes, sir."

"You look pale. What happened?"

"I was charged by a tiger."

"Where did this happen?"

"On the Plains."

"What were you doing—a spot of private tiger hunting?"

"No, sir. I was on my way home when it came for me out of the long grass. It came straight at me otherwise you may be sure I'd have left it alone. I had to shoot."

"What on earth was a tiger doing there?"

"I don't know, sir. I've never seen one there before."

"Did you kill it?"

"Unfortunately no. But I wounded it. I saw the blood. Perhaps that's why the charge was not fully maintained. At the last moment it swerved and went past me."

"Where did it go?"

"Into that strip of jungle on the lower side of the grass."

"Is it still there?"

"I think so. I heard it growling and crashing about just before I came on home. I was glad to get away."

James' father looked serious. "This is bad. A wounded tiger can be the very devil. Something will have to be done about it or we shall have trouble. I'll send out word to warn people to keep well clear of the Plains and attend to the business in the morning, which will allow time for the tiger's wound to stiffen. Go and drink a glass of water. You look as if you need it. You must have had a lucky escape."

"Yes, sir. Very lucky."

James had started to walk on when there was a rattle of hooves and Captain Lovell, on a riding pony, pulled up. With a wave and a cheerful greeting he dismounted.

"Where are you bound for?" inquired James' father.

"Nowhere in particular," was the answer. "I'm just riding round trying to gather information about a tiger."

"What tiger?"

"The one that's been making a nuisance of itself at Delapur."

"What's it been up to?"

"It started by taking goats, which itself is a bit unusual, but more recently it killed a woman cutting grass near the village. I went along hoping to get a crack at it, because, as you know, once they get a taste for that sort of meat they keep on. When I got to the village I was told the tiger hadn't been seen for some days, nor its pug marks at the pool where it habitually drinks. It must have moved, and I've been riding round looking for someone who may have seen it."

"Funny you should say that. James bumped

into a tiger within the last hour. He was walking across that piece of waste land we call the Plains when he says it made an unprovoked attack."

"Did he kill it?"

"Unfortunately no. But he fired three shots and must have hit it because he saw blood spots on the grass where it made off. I was about to make arrangements to finish it off when you turned up."

The Skipper looked at James, who had stood listening to the conversation. "Were you close to the tiger—close enough to get a good look at it?"

James smiled without humour. "Was I close? Too jolly close. It nearly knocked me down. If it had pressed home its charge I was a gonner; but for some reason at the last moment it swerved past me and went on into the cover of some jungle."

The Skipper nodded. "I've known them do that. I fancy it's because at the last instant, if the man doesn't move, they lose their nerve. My reason for asking if you had a close view was this: did you notice anything unusual about it?"

"No. I can't say I did. To me it looked like any other tiger."

"You didn't notice if it had any difficulty in walking?"

"Yes. Now you mention it. Before it charged it seemed to walk with a limp."

"That's interesting," the Skipper said. "Unless there are two limping tigers about it sounds as if you met the fellow I've been after. An old man in the village told me he thought it had a thorn in its foot. That would account for its bad behaviour. You'll have to do something about it, Bigglesworth, or you're likely to have man-eater trouble."

"I shall go after him in the morning," said James' father. "That will allow time for the wound to stiffen and for me to get some beaters together."

"If you can put me up for the night I'll stay and give you a hand if you like."

"Thanks. Much obliged. Stay by all means. Two guns can cover more ground than one."

"Why not let young James here make a third gun?"

"No." James' father was emphatic. "This is no business for a lad of his age."

"Oh please let me come, sir," pleaded James.

"No. That's final."

"I'm not asking to shoot. Just let me watch, please. I'll keep out of the way. There's a good tree on the track overlooking the Plains. I've climbed it before. I could sit there and see everything. After all, it was my tiger to start with."

"Oh very well. If you hit the tiger hard it may be dead by now. You can watch if you leave your rifle at home and promise not to leave the tree."

"I promise. Thank you, sir," agreed James joyfully.

When he got up the next morning it was to find preparations for the hunt well forward. About a dozen Gonds had assembled in the garden. It was their unpleasant task to drive the tiger from cover into the open. They were unarmed. Instead of a weapon each man carried an old bucket or a tin can of some sort, anything to make as much noise as possible. These men knew they would be taking their lives in their hands, but for that they were prepared; anything to get even with their hereditary enemy. Each man knew the ground and what was required of him.

There was no delay. The entire party moved off quietly, James' father and the Skipper going in front to put the beaters into position. James made for his tree and took up a comfortable position in a forked branch from which he had a clear view of the scene of operations.

Presently his father and the Skipper arrived alone. They took places about fifty yards apart and the same distance from the belt of jungle. This they faced, rifles ready. James regarded them with admiration. They seemed so unconcerned although they knew that at any moment their lives would depend on quick and accurate shooting. They stood clear in the open. There was no way of escape should the tiger charge, as it probably would when it saw them. With a twinge of anxiety James began to hope the tiger would be found dead.

He admired the courage of the Gond beaters still more. They knew that should the angry tiger turn back on them instead of breaking cover one of them at least would be badly mauled, probably killed. A piece of stick was no weapon to fight a tiger. They knew the risks and were prepared to accept them, not so much for the relatively small sum of money they would be paid as the satisfaction of seeing their hated enemy, now a public menace, laid low. They also knew that the widow of a man killed would be taken care of. Again, perhaps this was an opportunity to demonstrate their nerve.

James' father blew a long shrill blast on the whistle he carried. Instantly from the far side of the strip of jungle there broke out a tremendous din of yells and the banging of tin cans as the beaters advanced. The hunt was on.

Nearly breathless from excitement James watched. This, he thought, was real hunting. Not the killing of a fox or a badger but a creature that could, and would, fight back. He never forgot the picture of his father standing there, cool, calm and collected, waiting for striped death to emerge. Did this have any effect on the life he was to lead a few years later when he himself would be going out daily to meet death in a very different form, in the air? Possibly. No doubt it set a standard that he would feel he had to live up to.

The uproar continued, gradually drawing nearer.

James stared, his heart thumping in his chest. It nearly stopped beating when he saw the face of the tiger, just the face, appear in the fringe of shrubs straight in front of his father. But it was withdrawn instantly, as if the animal had realized the danger confronting it.

Apparently the Skipper had seen it, too, for he called: "Mark forward."

James' father raised a hand to show that he had seen the tiger.

Inside the jungle the din rose to a wild crescendo. Had the tiger broken back on the beaters? Never did James admire human courage more than at this moment; the sheer bravery of the men who were meeting a killer tiger on its own ground.

Then, in a flash, the tiger was there. It did not creep out. It burst out, tail lashing, fangs bared, a picture of snarling fury. It saw James' father and hated him on sight. It charged. James, fascinated by the sight, heard the report of his father's rifle. One shot. It was enough. With a terrible roar the tiger leapt high into the air, to fall tearing at the grass with its claws as it tried to get up. Its struggles ceased and it lay still.

The Skipper called: "Good shot, Bigglesworth. Great work." An expression James often used later.

James' father blew several short blasts on his whistle, and then, shouting to the beaters to stand back as they appeared in the thicket, he advanced towards the tiger, rifle still at the ready in case it should get up. He went close to the king of the jungle and put a bullet through its brain. Then he blew his whistle in a signal that it was all over.

The Gonds, cheering, ran up to tell the dead beast what they thought of it, and its ancestors. Some revealed their feelings by kicking the life-less body; and if this might be thought unsporting let it not be forgotten that they had no reason to have any respect for tigers—anyway, not dead ones.

James, as excited as the natives, dropped out of his tree and raced for the spot. He arrived at the same time as the Skipper, who pointed to one of the tiger's paws. It was badly swollen. Stooping, he withdrew a barbed porcupine quill and held it up. "This is what caused the mischief," he said. "The poor brute must have suffered agonies with this thing through his foot. Look, it was already turning septic. It would have killed him in the long run."

"Not before he would have killed several more people, so he's better out of the way," said James' father, unmoved by sympathy. "He has only himself to blame. He should have had more sense than to fool about with a porcupine."

An examination of the body revealed that two of James' shots had struck it, although neither was likely to prove fatal. One had scored along its ribs, and the other, entering the mouth, had torn a strip of skin off the side of its face as it came out. That, no doubt, was the shot James had fired point blank, and may have caused the swerve.

That was the end. The body of the tiger was carried off in triumph by the beaters, doubtless to have its whiskers cut off and some of its fat removed, the first for a lucky charm, and the second boiled down for ointment which (it is believed) is an infallible cure for rheumatism.

James would have said the beaters deserved it.

This was probably the tiger James had in mind when, some time afterwards, he was interviewed by the Headmaster on reporting to his school in England. At the same interview the Head said: "I believe you got a leopard, saving a man's life." To which James answered: "It was nothing, sir. He was an old man and the leopard went for his goat. I happened to come along with a rifle." So James made light of an incident which, as the following chapter will show, was not quite the simple affair he implied.

THE LAST ADVENTURE

THE morning came when James, now fourteen years of age, was informed by his father that his passage to England had been arranged so he had better start putting together the things he would like to take with him.

The intention at this stage of his life was that he should go to his father's old school before going on to university to study for the stiff Indian Civil Service examination in order to follow his father's profession. As we know, this did not happen. Long before the necessary time had elapsed his father had died and the world was tearing itself to pieces in the most ferocious war it had ever known; and inevitably James found himself involved in it. Thereafter his career ran on very different lines from the one he had anticipated. The same thing happened, of course, to countless other boys of his age—those who were lucky enough to survive. Twenty years later history was to repeat itself in a Second World War.

But to return to India.

Shaken by the news that he was soon to say good-bye to the life, and the friends, he had always known, with his rifle slung over his shoulder James wandered, deep in thought and a little sad, up the hill track to

THE LAST ADVENTURE 173

the tea estate to let his friend, Sula Dowla, know that they would be having no more excursions together as he would soon be on his way to England.

He reached the path leading to the bungalow where Sula lived with his parents, to meet him just going out. He carried a hatchet.

James said: "Where are you going?"

Sula answered: "Up the hill."

"What for?"

"To fetch an orchid."

James looked surprised. "An *orchid*! What do you want an orchid for?" His surprise was understandable because orchids of many sorts were as common as are moon-daisies in England.

With a roguish smile Sula explained. Out for a walk the previous day with Habu Din they had come on a branch that had fallen across the track. Growing on it was an exceptionally fine orchid plant. Habu had declared his intention of returning the following day to cut off the plant and tie it on a tree in his own garden.* To make a long story short, Sula said he was going to fetch the plant, not because he really wanted it but for a joke, to see the expression on Habu's face when he discovered the orchid had gone.

James did not think this was much of a joke but he did not say so. Anyway, there was no harm in it.

---

* This must have been one of the exotic epiphytic orchids that live on the bark of trees and do not require to have their roots in the ground, obtaining what food and moisture they need by hanging out air roots. They are common in tropical India.

This was the purpose of the hatchet. "How far is this branch?" he asked.

"Not far."

"I'll come with you," James said. "I have some news for you. After a little while I don't suppose I shall ever see you again." As they walked on slowly up the track he explained what was going to happen to him.

Sula looked sad. "I shall miss you," he said.

"When I go I will give you my rifle for a parting gift, but don't tell anybody about it," promised James.

"It won't be the same without you," Sula said in a melancholy voice. "We have only to go round the next bend so let us sit down here and you can tell me more about it. We shall see Habu if he comes. He can have the orchid. I don't want it now." They sat on a bank in a cool, shady spot. "What will you shoot in England?" inquired Sula.

James shrugged. "Nothing, I suppose."

"Why not?"

"For one thing there's nothing to shoot except birds. There is no hunting that you and I understand."

"No tigers?"

"No."

"Leopards, perhaps?"

"Not even leopards, nor bears, nor wild pigs."

"Then what do people hunt in England? They must hunt something."

"They hunt foxes."

"Foxes!" Sula looked incredulous. "Not much fun in that."

"Some people think so. Anyhow, there's nothing else."

"What a dull country. Why don't you stay here where there is always something to do?"

"My father says I must go to school. Besides, if I stay here I shall probably die of fever. Every time I have an attack it gets worse."

"Can't the doctor cure you?"

"No."

"I have some tiger fat. I'll give you some to rub on yourself. That will cure anything," declared Sula confidently.

"The doctor says the only thing that will cure me is different air. Cold air."

"Cold air will kill you," stated Sula. "Besides, it is so uncomfortable."

"No doubt I shall find it so until I get used to it," admitted James, lugubriously. "But don't let's talk about it. One day I'll come back. Then we shall be grown up and you can be my *shikari*. Meantime I may be able to find something to shoot at."

They fell silent. Little could James have imagined at that moment the sort of shooting in which he would be engaged before he saw India again: nor how long that would be.

As they sat there, pensive, suddenly the hush of the forest was shattered by such a clamour that the boys stared at each other in startled amazement. Monkeys whooped and screamed, birds cackled, and with the noise of the uproar came the frenzied voice of a man yelling and the wild bleating of a panic-stricken goat.

For a brief moment the boys stared at each other. They sprang to their feet. "Someone is in trouble," said James tersely.

"It's up here, just round the corner," Sula said, and raced on up the track.

"Wait!" shouted James, prudently.

But either Sula did not hear, or took no notice, so he ran after him, trying to unsling his rifle as he ran. This of course impeded him, and Sula reached the bend first. He saw him falter, beckon furiously, and go on to disappear round the bend.

James reached it to see a sight he would have found difficult to imagine. The track ran through a little open glade. In the middle of it an old man appeared to be having a wrestling match with a leopard. Man and beast were staggering about, the leopard on its hind legs; the man, with an arm locked round its neck, was holding its back tight against his chest either in the hope of strangling the animal or to prevent its teeth and claws from getting at his body. Such clothes as he wore were already in shreds. Sula was dancing round the pair of them brandishing his hatchet, looking for somewhere to strike. More than that he could not do for fear of hitting the man. The only place where he could do the leopard any serious harm with a small hatchet was its head, but as this was in conjunction with the man's face it was obvious that if he struck he was just as likely to brain the man as the animal. They were not still for a moment. Actually, the old man, in his desperation, was tearing at the back of the leopard's head with his teeth, although the only purpose this served was to drive it into an insane fury. Close at hand a goat was rushing about as if demented. The noise was indescribable.

James joined in the mêlée; but of course he was as helpless to do anything as Sula, for the same reason. He had his rifle free, but as man and beast tottered about this way and that, locked in a life-or death embrace, to shoot at the leopard without a grave risk of hitting the man was just not possible. Utter confusion reigned.

The old man gasped: "Shoot—shoot."

James daren't risk it. All he could do was jab the leopard in the stomach with the muzzle of the rifle shouting, "Let it go."

Whether the man obeyed or lost his grip was not clear—probably the latter, for he was at his last gasp, eyes staring and foam on his lips. At all events the leopard fell clear. Now on all fours it sprang at Sula, making a swipe with a bunch of claws which, had they reached Sula's face, would have left him without one. Sula parried the blow with his hatchet, but the force of it sent him reeling backwards. The leopard, spinning round, then leapt at the old man and knocked him sprawling. It was on him in a flash. Before James could get in a shot, Sula, who appeared to have gone mad too, jumped in and made a wild swipe at the animal's

head with his hatchet. The blow landed on the
leopard's neck, where it did little harm on account
of the thick hair, through which the edge could
not penetrate. The blade was probably blunt,
anyway.

It is easier to imagine the scene than to describe it.
Everyone was shouting, but no one really knew
what he was doing. That included the snarling,
spitting leopard. It turned back on Sula and
crouched to spring. This gave James the chance for
which he had been waiting. He jumped in, and
with the muzzle of the rifle almost touching the
leopard's shoulder, fired. The leopard leapt high
into the air, came down on its back and lay kicking.
For a few seconds it twitched convulsively, tearing
up the grass with its claws. James fired two more
bullets into it and all was over.

The only sound now came from the old man. He
was making incoherent noises but at least he was
on his feet. James leaned against a tree, breathless,
sweat pouring down his face. Sula sank down,
panting, exhausted. From first to last the whole
thing could not have lasted more than three minutes;
but what it lacked in time was made up for by the
intensity of the action.

After he had recovered somewhat, James went to
the old man to see how badly he had been hurt. To
his surprise he found him unharmed except for a
few superficial scratches. The old man called his
goat, which ran to him. James looked at the
leopard. It was only a small one, evidently a young

one; which was lucky for the old man, probably for all of them.

Then, sitting on the ground, the old man told the boys what had happened. Lachme—that was the name of the goat—was an old nanny which in her ripe age had become a pet, living in the house with the family. She was allowed to roam free, but had become stupid, wandering farther than was wise. That was what had happened this morning. Fearing for her safety, the old man said, he had gone to find her and bring her home. It was while he was doing this that the leopard had charged out of the jungle and tried to seize her.

The old man went to her rescue, whereupon the leopard had turned on him. Having no weapon, for he was not expecting anything like this to happen so near home, he had seized the leopard round the neck and tried to choke it to death. In this he failed, but having got a grip he daren't let go. That was the situation when the boys had arrived on the scene. He thanked them for their timely intervention, as, indeed, he had good reason.

In case the credulity of the reader should be strained by the idea of a man fighting a leopard with his bare hands it is on record that this has more than once been done successfully, in Africa as well as India, although of course not from choice but as a last resort on being attacked. The men concerned did not always recover from their injuries, dying later as a result of their wounds turning septic. The teeth and claws of all flesh-eating animals, and this includes cats and dogs, if they draw blood, can be poisonous, and highly dangerous if not dealt with quickly.

Well, that was the end of the affair with a young leopard which took on more than he could manage.

James and Sula were still sitting there talking about it when Habu arrived, also carrying a chopper, on his way to collect the orchid. It is hardly necessary to say he was amazed at what had happened. James left them to collect the orchid (although, understandably, Sula professed to have no further interest in it) and returned home.

Three weeks later he was on his way to England, where there were no tigers or leopards—anyway, not wild ones.

IN CONCLUSION

Not by the widest stretch of the imagination could young James Bigglesworth (or anyone else of his age) have foreseen the momentous events that were to rock the world in a single lifetime; wars that were to reshape countries, change the colours on nearly every page of the atlas and make geography, as it was then taught, as out of date as the prehistoric monsters that once roamed the earth. Men were striving to reach the Poles as they now grope for the moon. Some countries have vanished, their original inhabitants with them, or changed out of recognition. New ones have been created, new capital cities established, great areas renamed.

What in Biggles' early days were blanks on the map now have teeming populations. Native tribal chiefs in what was called "Darkest Africa" now ride in motor cars. Mud huts have been replaced with palaces and skyscrapers that house refrigerators and television sets. All this in a lifetime. These changes must be borne in mind when reading the Biggles books, particularly the earlier ones.

As it has not been practicable to change the place names in the many books the original ones remain, and the reader must adjust himself accordingly.

No less astonishing have been scientific and

technical development. When Biggles was a boy "penny-farthing" bicycles were still on the road. A new vehicle called an automobile had to be preceded by a man with a red flag. There were no aeroplanes. Even when on leaving school he learned to fly, a speed of seventy mile san hour was the limit. Against a head wind a plane could make little, if any, progress. None carried more than two people. They had this advantage. In an emergency they could land almost anywhere; which was just as well, for structural and engine failure were common and aerodromes few and far between. There were no passenger services, no radio, much less television. What from a schoolboy's view was more important, however, was that a penny would buy a quarter of a pound of chocolates or other sweets.

The reader has only to look around to see the changes, even in the way of thought, that grew up with Biggles.